SEVENTH HEAVEN

Riding high on her promotion as a tour representative in Bermuda, Juliet Hamilton is soon brought down to earth by Reece Carter, the arrogant proprietor of the luxurious Island Cove Hotel. He reminds her that the rich clientele who haunt his hotel are a far cry from the average tourist with whom she has previously had dealings. His reminder becomes a stark fact when one of his most revered guests accuses Juliet of stealing — but who will Reece believe?

Books by Margaret Astridge
in the Linford Romance Library:

STAR OF ARGENCE

MARGARET ASTRIDGE

SEVENTH HEAVEN

Complete and Unabridged

LINFORD
Leicester
27979

First published in Great Britain in 1993 by
Robert Hale Limited
London

First Linford Edition
published February 1995
by arrangement with
Robert Hale Limited
London

British Library CIP Data

Astridge, Margaret
    Seventh heaven.—Large print ed.—
    Linford romance library
    I. Title II. Series
    823.914 [F]

    ISBN 0–7089–7666–2

Published by
F. A. Thorpe (Publishing) Ltd.
Anstey, Leicestershire

Set by Words & Graphics Ltd.
Anstey, Leicestershire
Printed and bound in Great Britain by
T. J. Press (Padstow) Ltd., Padstow, Cornwall

This book is printed on acid-free paper

1

THE Island Cove Hotel stood majestic and white, like a modern day palace, in forty lush acres of semi-tropical gardens. Overlooking a picturesque cove with a beautiful expanse of pink coral beach, this magnificent hotel — a resort in its own right — was undoubtedly one of the most luxurious of its genre. Juliet Hamilton was astounded that Ultimate Tours should have put her in charge of the one hundred or so British tourists now languishing in such opulence.

"Impressive, isn't it?" commented a warm and friendly English voice at her right shoulder. "Wait until you see the other side — the terraces and the gardens that go right down to the beach."

Juliet spun round, coming face to face with a blond, well-bronzed man not much older than herself. He was dressed informally in white open-necked shirt and shorts, and the bright, early morning sun that was just rising enhanced his even tan.

"Have you just arrived?" he enquired, eyeing the large suitcase standing by her legs.

Juliet looked about her with a sense of disorientation. "I think so! I've come from southern Spain via Madrid, London and New York. I started out twenty-four hours ago and I'm not quite sure whether I'm still travelling or I've actually arrived. My head's spinning."

His laugh was gentle and ringing with sympathy. "With such a demanding travel schedule you're obviously not a tourist on holiday."

"No, unfortunately. I'm the representative for Ultimate Tours."

"Ah," — the light dawned on his face — "you must be taking the place of Jane Tyson who was posted to Hawaii a few days ago. I'm Jan Peters, sports coach — swimming, tennis, scuba diving and generally pampering to the whims and fancies of the wealthy cretins who mistakenly think they're in the peak of condition. Do you know, Bermuda is about the only place in the world where you don't have to slim before visiting it. Americans make up most of the tourist influx — and they're all huge."

Juliet marvelled at his outspoken description of the clientele who haunted such places as the Island Cove Hotel. She understood the point he was making but her loyalty to her job and to Ultimate Tours meant her own sentiments remained securely closeted away.

"Juliet Hamilton," she told him, extending her hand and feeling it encased in a warm and friendly grasp.

"Fancy a coffee? None of the restaurants are open yet but the kitchen staff are around."

"I don't think so, thank you all the same. I'm really so tired."

"Yes, you must be. Do you know

where you're living?"

"Haven't a clue. The taxi dropped me here. I was just on my way to reception."

"You'll probably be staying in the same bungalow Jane had, on the beach side of the hotel. It's a fair way to walk. Why don't you make your way over and I'll go and wake up the night staff at reception."

Sheer exhaustion and an uncharacteristic lethargy enticed her to accept his proposal.

"That's so kind of you. Thank you," she said, reaching down to pick up her suitcase.

"No, leave that," he told her. "I'll take it to reception and get one of the porters to carry it over. That's what they're paid for."

Too weary to protest she thanked Jan again and took the path he had indicated, around the side of the hotel building and through the lush park where small white bungalows were semi-hidden between flower-strewn

4

bushes. Most of the pale blue window shutters were closed indicating that the occupants were still asleep. It served to remind her of the early hour, and a glance at her watch confirmed that it was almost five o'clock in the morning. It could have been the beginning of August. Or was it still July? And as for the day of the week she couldn't even guess — Wednesday, Thursday, Friday? She groaned at the recollection of the long and wearying journey she had just undertaken.

What could she say about her job? At the moment there wasn't a lot to recommend it. Did it fall short of her expectations? No, not really, although she often worked above and beyond the call of duty. She liked meeting people, an important requisite for the job, and the possibility of travelling to exotic places had been instrumental in guiding her towards such a career.

For the past two years, though, she had been closeted in a Spanish resort on one of the costas, with six medium-class hotels to supervise and hundreds of British tourists who overdid their sunbathing and constantly complained about the lack of fish and chips and pots of tea on the menu.

It was where the company usually sent their newly-trained reps, for there was no better place on earth to study and understand the needs of the Briton in a foreign habitat.

After the obligatory tour of duty, a rep could look forward to postings farther afield, where the clientele was more discerning. The opulence and luxury of the Far East havens and the Caribbean were reserved for those long-term reps with several years' experience under their belts of handling the wealthiest of tourists.

So Juliet's sudden posting to Seventh Heaven, as the Bermudans liked to call the numerous islands, after just two years with the company, was totally unusual and unexpected. She could only think that Ultimate Tours were short-staffed and that she was the only rep available for immediate transfer.

Jan caught her up just as she was enjoying the first glimpse of the coral beach with its coconut matting umbrellas and the sea sparkling between each one. A porter brought up the rear, striding out manfully with her suitcase.

"I thought it would be Jane's bungalow," Jan said. "I've got the key. Come on and I'll show you where it is."

"Did you know Jane well?" Juliet queried.

"Well enough to be able to take you to her bungalow," he said wickedly.

Walking a couple of paces behind Jan, Juliet ran a probing glance over him. Of medium height and slim build with muscular limbs, she could well imagine that this attractive young sports coach had a way with the ladies; and she wasn't too tired to suspect that his roving eye had already singled her out for a future dalliance.

A few minutes later Jan stopped in front of a small, low, one storey building painted white, with the obligatory blue shutters at the windows. He unlocked the door for her and stepped back to allow her through.

"Here we are," he announced. "Just a bedroom, bathroom and small kitchenette. Not luxurious but adequate."

And it was. Comfortably fitted out with cane furniture Juliet found it very agreeable. Everything in the room was either blue or white or both, and frilly; and the French windows which led out onto a small but private patio were quite delightful.

The porter came in with her suitcase and Jan slipped him a tip, waving away Juliet's offer to repay him.

"I suppose you're too tired to take a wander round the grounds and across to the hotel? I could show you where everything is then you won't appear too lost and confused when the guests ask you questions."

It was a superb idea of Jan's to help her familiarize herself with her new surroundings, but she really must try and snatch a few hours' sleep.

"Another time," she replied with a helpless shrug. "There is another rep here, isn't there?"

"Yes, there are several. American, French and of course Alison Gregory, the other Ultimate rep. She's based at the Coral Reef hotel, about five miles along the coast. She'll probably pop over and introduce herself later today. I'll leave you to catch up on your sleep then. See you around."

Juliet was so tired that she decided to leave her suitcase until later. After a very quick shower she climbed into bed exhausted, and managed a few hours' fitful sleep.

She was woken finally by a persistent knocking at the door to the bungalow. It took her a few moments to come round, but she gathered her scattered thoughts and with head spinning stumbled unsteadily to the door. A flood of glittering sunlight greeted her along with a young woman in the familiar red, white and blue striped dress that was the uniform for Ultimate reps.

"Juliet?" she queried. "Juliet Hamilton?"

Even in her dishevelled state of mind Juliet sensed the agitation in the tone of the other. She blinked the sleep from her eyes and pushed a hand back through her tousled chestnut hair that tumbled and curled in chaotic confusion over her face and shoulders.

"Yes, that's me."

"I came an hour ago but there was no reply. I've been knocking ages. I'm Alison Gregory, the other Ultimate rep."

"Oh, hello." Juliet finally began to come to. "Do you want to come in?"

"I'd like to but I can't. Didn't you know you were supposed to be on duty at 10.30 this morning? To welcome the new batch of guests from the UK."

Any remnants of sleep were wiped away as a cold horror crept over her.

She glanced at her watch. It showed midday exactly.

"I . . . I'd no idea," she gasped. "I only arrived at five, this morning."

A notable look of fellow-feeling swept over Alison's face. "Poor you," she murmured sympathetically. "Didn't you check the duty rota in the foyer when you checked in?"

"I didn't check in," Juliet told her. "Jan Peters did it for me. Oh, help!" Her top teeth nibbled at her bottom lip. "Am I in trouble?"

"Alan Scarlet's not too pleased. He wants to see you."

"Alan Scarlet?" Juliet repeated. "I thought the hotel was run by Reece Carter."

Alison's laugh brought a more favourable atmosphere that helped ease Juliet's fraught state.

"Oh, you really don't know the place at all, do you? Reece Carter owns the hotel, or at least his parents do. Alan Scarlet runs it. He's the manager. He supervises the hotel like a commanding ficer in the army and can't bear any deviation from routine. So you'd better hurry on over before he blows a gasket. Look, I'm sorry we had to meet like this. I'll catch you later and then we can get to know each other better."

It took Juliet just five minutes to drag the obligatory striped dress from her suitcase and arrange her hair into a more presentable style; then she hurried from the bungalow and along the meandering paths to the hotel.

It was a different world to that she had experienced at five that morning. The gardens were alive with guests making their way to and from the beach. The rhythmic lobbing of a ball suggested that the tennis courts were close by, and in the distance shouts and screams could be heard from the area around the swimming pools.

Most of the holiday makers were of an older generation, but there were those couples obviously on honeymoon, and a number of children darted around the paths, too. Then there was the usual

12

bevy of ravishing creatures that always decorated the beaches and gardens of such sumptuous establishments. It didn't pass Juliet's notice that some of these young women were accompanied by men old enough to be their fathers or even their grandfathers.

The spacious and sumptuous foyer of the hotel offered an air-conditioned coolness that chilled Juliet's nervous body. At this time of the day it was busy with people queueing at the bureau de change and others crowding around the reception desk waiting for the keys to their rooms so that they could change for lunch.

Through this mass of sun-reddened, over-heated bodies she edged her way to the front.

"Where can I find Mr Scarlet?" she asked a young woman smartly dressed in a lightweight navy blue suit.

"Down the corridor, over there," she said, waving vaguely in the direction of the opposite side of the foyer.

Juliet pushed her way back through

the conflicting smells of suntan lotions that were assailing her nostrils, and hurried down the corridor that led off from one side of the foyer. At the far end an unmarked door stood slightly ajar, and from within came the clack-clack of a typewriter. Juliet pushed the door open cautiously and walked in. A secretary was tapping away impressively at a typewriter. She looked up and smiled as Juliet appeared.

"I'm Juliet Hamilton, the representative for Ultimate Tours. I understand Mr Scarlet wants to see me."

"Oh, yes, Miss Hamilton. I'm afraid he does. Your absence caused quite a kerfuffle here, this morning, what with the new arrivals having no Ultimate Tours rep to welcome them."

"I didn't know I was supposed to be on duty," Juliet explained.

The secretary smiled sympathetically. "Arrived late, did you?"

Juliet groaned. "Five hours late."

"Oh, dear! The wonders of modern travel! Go right in, will you? Mr Scarlet will be with you just as soon as he can."

Juliet wiped her perspiring hands down the sides of her dress and went through the door the secretary had indicated. At the same time, from an ante room, a man emerged into the large office, tall, dark-looking, in his early thirties. He was wiping his hands on a towel but stopped on seeing her and gave her a brief but thorough once-over.

Juliet sensed he wasn't just anybody. The cut of his traditional mid-grey suit and white shirt hinted that he held a high position in the hotel. She guessed that this man was Alan Scarlet and felt apprehensive, afraid even, which made her ignore the warm, easy smile that slowly crept over his face.

Juliet decided to get in first with her explanation.

"I'm Juliet Hamilton. I can explain everything. I spent two hours on a crowded train travelling from the south of Spain to Madrid because there was no room on the chartered holiday flights. At Madrid airport I had to wait three hours for a plane that was delayed an hour because of engine trouble. Finally I arrived in London where I had to wait yet another four hours for the connecting flight to New York. The flight from New York to Bermuda was on time but took an hour longer than usual because of strong head winds and turbulence. I actually arrived here in Bermuda at three o'clock in the morning, had a lot of trouble finding a taxi at that unearthly hour, and was finally deposited in front of this hotel just seven hours ago."

Having had her little say she fell silent, expecting similar sympathetic murmurings to those that Jan, Alison and the secretary had bestowed on her. She waited for words that would suggest there had been a misunderstanding, that no, she could hardly have been expected to be on duty after such arduous travel. None came.

He tossed the towel down carelessly

onto a chair and moved into the room to stand in front of the window. There was no longer even a hint of a smile playing on his lips.

"That was quite an opening line, Miss Hamilton." His voice was quiet yet as dry as autumn leaves. "We all have our crosses to bear. I'm sorry you think yours is worse than anyone else's."

A crimson flush spread up Juliet's neck and into her face on realizing she had overdone her little piece. She remained silent in the face of his quiet reprimand and her own embarrassment.

"Mr Scarlet's not here at the moment. He's been called away. But whatever you've done to incur his wrath he will deal with it. Actually I came along to welcome you. I'm Reece Carter."

2

UNTIL that moment Juliet had been too preoccupied with the reprimand to come and her own defence to notice her surroundings. Now she gradually overcame the shock and for the first time became aware of the room and the man dominating it.

The walls and woodwork were painted white, and the ceiling was of fancy plasterwork in a pattern of palm leaves. A light hung from the centre on a brass chain that could be lowered or highered, but so much daylight poured in through the three floor-length windows that it was doubtful any artificial light was needed, except at night.

A bookcase filled one wall, its shelves packed with blue bound volumes large enough to be the hotel ledgers from days before computers accommodated the filing system. There were other books too; dictionaries — English, French and German — books on travel, books on Bermuda, books about the Caribbean. There was also a rather attractive oil painting of a young woman in her early twenties, and even though Juliet had never seen the woman before she suspected that the artist had captured the very essence of her serene personality. She wore a white floral summer dress cut on the lines of the fashion of the early fifties and in one hand she carried a matching head scarf.

It was, without exception, a man's room, with Bermudan cedar and a large solid desk dominating it. Through the windows, behind Reece Carter, a private, walled garden shimmered in the noonday sun. An old gardener in a large, battered straw hat made a very lethargic attempt at hoeing the soil.

"You're very young to be representing Ultimate Tours here in Bermuda, Miss Hamilton." Reece Carter moved away from the window, walked round the desk and perched himself on one corner. "Please sit down."

Juliet did so, piqued that he should find it necessary to comment upon her age and inexperience.

"I've completed all my training," she retorted. "And Ultimate Tours would hardly choose someone who wasn't suited to the type of clientele who stay at the Island Cove Hotel."

He ran an assessing glance over her from head to toe then examined her for a few pensive seconds. There was nothing insulting in his study, it was even rather impersonal and tinged with a hauteur that made Juliet's hair stand on end.

"Tell me, Miss Hamilton, what kind of clientele is that?"

With difficulty Juliet swallowed over a dry throat. She could have murdered a glass of water for she was dehydrated from travelling.

"Well . . . " she began hesitantly, her thoughts hovering around Jan Peters' disrespectful references to wealthy cretins dripping with money. Quickly she pushed them away. "Many of the guests are British. The Island Cove Hotel is very popular with British visitors because of its range of facilities and its value for money. There is a similarity to the hotels in Spain where I worked for the past two years."

Her diplomatic and careful reply seemed to satisfy him, for a smile, albeit a cool one, passed across his lips. In the short silence that followed she was able to make a quick assessment of this man who owned the hotel that had recently made it into the world's top twenty most luxurious hotels list.

He wasn't handsome by conventional standards, but there was no denying the good looks of the proprietor of the Island Cove Hotel. He was a tall, sensuous-looking man, his body lean, his skin bronzed, and he had the kind of deep, quiet timbre to his voice that made a person sit up and take notice.

His mid-Atlantic accent was neither

especially attractive nor remarkable, but he had the trick of speaking without any hesitations, and this lent an air of authority to him which made it easy to believe in his determination to get what he wanted.

There was something fierce, stubborn and resolute about him. Juliet could sense it without even knowing him, and a ripple of fear almost, ran through her as he continued his study of her.

"Hmmm," he murmured eventually, obviously still not entirely sold on Ultimate Tours' choice of representative. "The Island Cove Hotel is a first class hotel, Miss Hamilton. It has a long-established reputation for popularity, especially amongst British guests. We have many facilities including several restaurants, bars, night-club, shops, beauty salon and health club, along with three freshwater pools — one solely for the use of children — six all-weather tennis courts and almost every watersport imaginable. Golf is also available. You can see that the

Island Cove is far superior to any hotel you have yet experienced." The ensuing short pause made all the more clear his doubts about her suitability. "Well, I suppose Miss Gregory will keep an eye on you. Are you comfortable in your bungalow?"

Furious that he was judging her on her age and inexperience she retorted dryly, "I haven't seen much of it yet."

"You probably won't see much of it anyway," he rejoindered. "Only the guests are here to relax and while away the hours in the sun."

At that point the door opened, and a man of around fifty, dark hair showing many signs of greying, poked his head through the opening.

"Oh, I'm sorry, Mr Carter. I didn't know you were busy."

"That's all right, Alan. Come in. This is Miss Hamilton, the representative for Ultimate Tours."

"Ah, yes, Miss Hamilton." He ran a disapproving and superior eye over her. "I'm Alan Scarlet, the hotel manager."

Juliet's anger evaporated and was replaced by nervousness. Her palms became clammy and she felt a fine sheen of perspiration erupt over her top lip. The manager was suave, well-groomed and dressed in cream Bermuda shorts, dark jacket, silk shirt and tie. Dark socks and shoes completed his immaculate outfit which projected assurance and sternness, as no doubt it was meant to do.

"Miss Hamilton failed to attend the welcoming reception for the new guests at 10.30 this morning," the manager explained to Reece Carter. "That left the reception desk inundated with twelve tired and demanding guests floundering in confusion."

Reece Carter's eyes deviated from the manager to Juliet's face and he studied her once more in sombre silence.

Juliet's anger resurfaced. For heaven's sake, anyone would think she had committed the crime of the decade. And *twelve* guests! That was nothing! In Spain she had had to deal with fifty at a time. And besides, apart from murdering a whingeing hotel guest, she was answerable to no one but Ultimate Tours. They were her employers, not Alan Scarlet, nor Reece Carter.

"Fortunately I was on hand to ease their queries," Alan Scarlet was saying. "And Miss Gregory also arrived shortly afterwards." He turned his superior gaze back to Juliet. "Not a very good start, Miss Hamilton. I hope this unreliability is not a sign of things to come."

A wave of distress now surged over Juliet. If there was one word that could never be used to describe her it was unreliable. She was keen and ambitious about her job, and took a great pride in doing it well. To be associated with laxity cut deep. She opened her mouth to protest but Reece Carter cut across her.

"I'm sure, Alan, that Miss Hamilton will take great pains to see that it doesn't happen again." The tone of his voice declared that that should be the end of the matter and it suddenly occurred to Juliet that Reece Carter had intervened on her behalf, so warding off the possibility of any more unpleasantness.

Alan Scarlet immediately obeyed the veiled hint to proceed no further. "I've arranged for you to meet the latest arrivals at four this afternoon, Miss Hamilton. Many are established guests who visit us every year and who have come to expect a high standard of efficiency which we intend to meet. Perhaps you'd be good enough to make your apologies and to help them settle in."

Juliet noticed that Alan Scarlet was still having a dig at her despite Reece Carter's intervention. She suspected that his reprimand would have been much stronger had Reece Carter not been present. Despite herself she found herself offering a silent vote of thanks to the hotel's owner.

Reece Carter glanced at his watch.

"So, you've got about three and three-quarter hours to get genned up on the hotel and what it offers. You might give a mention to the boat trips we organize around the bays; and this year we are trying out something new — an outing by air to the so-called Bermuda Triangle for our more intrepid guests. Could you make a special point of that?" He stood up, addressed himself to the manager. "I'm off for a spot of lunch now. Come and see me around two this afternoon, and we'll go over last month's figures."

"Certainly, Mr Carter." Alan Scarlet sounded almost obsequious, and even offered him a slight bow.

A shiver ran down Juliet's spine at his ingratiating manner. If there was one thing she found intolerable it was the servile attitude of one person to another. She stood up and moved towards the door which Reece Carter opened for her. Passing through the outer office then into the corridor she found the hotel's proprietor accompanying her towards the foyer.

"Have you notified Ultimate Tours of your arrival yet?" he asked. The grey eyes looked infinitely patronizing as he glanced down at her.

Juliet's hackles rose again. Because of her obvious youth and inexperience he was taking it upon himself to remind her to carry out her tasks — as one might a child. It so happened that she had had every intention of contacting the London office upon her arrival, but because she had been late and very tired she had deferred doing so until the morning.

"It's all in hand," she retorted tartly.

"Which means you haven't done it," he surmised. Once more he let his gaze stray from the bustling foyer to briefly rest on her, skimming over her. "You really must contact them, Miss Hamilton. Otherwise there'll be an anxious trans-Atlantic phone call from London asking if you've arrived and why you haven't checked in. Go to the reception and get them to put you through."

On these words he veered off and strode away across the foyer towards the main restaurant, like a man who expected his orders to be carried out. They probably were, too, Juliet decided sourly, moving towards the reception desk and realizing she was doing just that. She gritted her teeth and waited for one of the receptionists to attend to her.

"Excuse me."

A voice behind brought her out of her ill humour and she turned round. A middle-aged woman, small, well-built with an attractive, enquiring face peered up at her.

"Are you the representative for Ultimate Tours?"

Juliet's hand automatically went to her chest where she should have been displaying her badge of office. It wasn't there. She had put on a clean dress that morning and omitted to pin on her tag.

"Yes, I am. I've forgotten to put on my badge."

"I thought I recognized the striped dress. What's your name?"

"Juliet Hamilton. Have you a problem?"

"Just a small one. Our name is Fairweather. Mr and Mrs Archie Fairweather. When we booked we asked specifically for a ground floor room. We arrived this morning and found we had been given a room on the first floor. It's my husband, you see. He's in a wheelchair. I don't want to be any trouble but it would be so much more convenient if we could move to the ground floor."

Juliet's anger at Reece Carter's authoritative manner disintegrated as her caring nature came to the fore and she threw herself into the role of problem-solver. However it wasn't as straightforward as she thought. The reception staff were decidedly unhelpful. Whether it was because they sensed she was new and unfamiliar with the hotel, or whether they had had their fill of demanding guests, she didn't know. What she did know was that she was the representative for Ultimate Tours, that one of her clients had a genuine problem, and that she would persist until it was solved.

She demanded to see the registration cards the guests who had arrived that morning had filled out, scanned them to see who was the most likely to be able to change rooms, went along to their room to explain the situation to them, and by 1.30 the Fairweathers were installed in their new room on the ground floor. Their warm-hearted thanks and gratitude pushed away any of Juliet's remaining despondency and helped her rediscover her zest for her job.

Towards four o'clock that afternoon Juliet felt at a low ebb. She hadn't eaten since her last meal on the plane early that morning. An uncontrollable tiredness had come over her, and a headache was coming on in great thumping throbs. If only she could go to bed, slide between the cool sheets, and succumb to the beckoning relaxation.

She made herself a cup of tea in the kitchenette of her bungalow then ambled across to the hotel and one of the smaller lounges where Alan Scarlet had arranged for her to meet the new arrivals whom she should have welcomed that morning. Some were already there and the remaining few straggled in shortly afterwards.

Just as she was about to start her little welcoming speech the door opened and to her horror Reece Carter stepped in and installed himself at the back of the room. Folding his arms across his chest he stood there like an invigilator at the back of a classroom during an examination.

He was still wearing the grey suit and white shirt, all tailored to fit his frame perfectly. The effect was one of power and authority, and his stance displayed an ease in shouldering it.

Juliet stared at him, her thoughts

riotous in her throbbing head, and for a moment she lost her nerve. She was sure he was there to assess her performance. The silence lengthened. Her head throbbed. Twelve pairs of eyes peered at her expectantly, along with Reece Carter's dark grey gaze, veiled, unreadable.

She swallowed, offered her apologies for her absence that morning and asked if everyone had settled in. She told them she was new, that it was her first day at the Island Cove Hotel, and asked that they bear with her until she got into her stride. She avoided meeting Reece Carter's unwavering stare. Mrs Fairweather smiled sympathetically and Juliet experienced a welcome, if brief, moment of renewed confidence.

She went on to inform the guests of meal times, of the hotel facilities, of the boat trips around the bay that could be arranged. At this point her willpower deserted her and she flicked a glance to the back of the room where Reece Carter still lingered, arms folded across his chest. His face was an expressionless mask, neither encouraging nor disapproving. She was clearly still on trial.

Nervously she ran her fingers back through her hair then flicked over the sheets fastened onto her clipboard. What had she forgotten? Oh, Lord! The blessed Bermuda Triangle outing by air! And he had asked her to make a special point of it. To her credit she neatly slipped it into her closing speech, separating it from the rest of the trips and giving it an importance of its own. Then she informed the guests when she would next be on duty and where they might find her.

Most of the guests stood up and ambled out of the lounge, chatting amongst themselves about the trips and deciding which ones to try. Others remained and queried her further on specific items, so for the next half-hour she hardly had time to look up from her clipboard. When she did, after the last guest had thanked her for her help and left, it was to find Reece Carter still at the back of the room. A sense of apprehension crept over her and she pressed her fingers fleetingly to her aching temple. Had she projected herself badly? Had she missed something? Why was he still there? And what was she doing worrying about it anyway? It was only making her headache worse.

Gathering her composure she collected her briefcase, clipboard and various papers and made her way briskly towards the door.

"You look very strained, Miss Hamilton," he commented.

"Doesn't everyone when they've just taken an examination?" Her gaze was averted, her voice stiff, her head held high. "Did I pass?"

"I suppose it could be termed passable," he conceded, although he didn't sound altogether enthusiastic. "I'm glad to see you've read up on Bermuda and the hotel."

"What else did you expect?" Irritation

emanated from her like an electric force field. "I've been posted here for the foreseeable future. It's in my own interests to know more than the guests."

"Really?" His dark eyebrows shot up in surprise, and his voice was heavy with sarcasm. "You're very fortunate. I've lived here in Bermuda all my life, and there are still some guests who know more than I do. Like the Fairweathers, for instance."

Juliet half pivoted round, coming face to face with him.

"The Fairweathers know everything there is to know about Bermuda," he went on. "They have been coming here every year for the past twenty years." He paused now — unusual for him — and the following silence seemed somehow contrived, as if he really didn't want to continue. "Mrs Fairweather mentioned to me about your help in securing a ground floor room for them. She spoke very highly of your politeness and your concern for

36

her problem, and asked that she might convey to you her thanks once more via myself."

Juliet was off guard, completely unprepared for such a gesture coming from the man who considered her too inexperienced to deal with the affluent clientele who haunted his hotel. She was also very aware that it had all been undertaken with a blatant reluctance. She was suddenly very angry as exhaustion and pain mingled beyond control.

"It is my job, Mr Carter. And whilst we're on the subject of politeness, maybe you could shake up your receptionists who were quite unhelpful with the Fairweathers. They are, after all, your employees."

His eyes narrowed but there was no response from him. Juliet felt a sense of elation. She had hit home, she could tell. She had found a flaw in his immaculately run hotel and he clearly didn't like it.

Now in her stride she pushed on,

falling back on her own authoritative position and using it to give vent to the anger bubbling inside her.

"As for myself, I am not employed by you. I'm an independent agent, representing a world-renowned tour company. We also have standards to meet. It's perhaps worth remembering that should I begin sending back reports about the couldn't-care-less attitude of your staff, Ultimate Tours might consider dropping the Island Cove Hotel from their brochures."

The tanned skin on his face flushed, and the dark grey of his eyes were like steel. Right now they also held a burning anger.

Juliet's sense of triumph blossomed almost to euphoria. It was possibly the best exit line she would ever have, and taking advantage of it she spun briskly on her heel and marched from the lounge.

She only went a few steps, though, when she felt her arm grasped, halting her abruptly.

"Just a moment, Miss Hamilton." His voice was low with anger but controlled. "Just who the *hell* do you think you are to criticize my hotel? Not one of the tour reps has ever found it necessary to find fault with it. In fact Miss Tyson's and Miss Gregory's politeness and amenability have always been exemplary." His eyes glittered with anger in his tanned face. "Yet you, Miss Hamilton — you who have come straight from some Spanish costa and are still wet behind the ears — within hours of your arrival here, you have the gall to accuse my staff of slackness."

"Maybe that's what the hotel needs. Someone to shake it out of its complacency." She spoke with the venom of sheer exhaustion and Reece Carter was not amused.

"Complacency!" His voice was a low roar that sent a tremor through Juliet. "My God, don't you know this hotel is amongst the best in the world? It has recently been given an award for all-round excellence by a panel of international judges far more experienced and knowledgeable than you."

Juliet was beginning to tremble, whether from anger or alarm she did not know. "Then I can only think that your staff made a supreme effort on the day the judges were here," she snapped back. "Believe me, this morning their attitude left much to be desired."

There was a stillness about him, a containment, a cold anger held in check. "It's your attitude, Miss Hamilton, that leaves much to be desired. Anyone who barges up to the reception desk at the busiest time of the day — yes, barges, Miss Hamilton. I have been informed of what happened — demanding immediate service when other guests are waiting to be attended to, deserves to be given the cold shoulder."

"Sometimes one has to push oneself forward to get results."

"My receptionists would have dealt

with your problem when the rush had died down. A little patience from yourself would have brought the results you wanted. Instead you made a scene, embarrassing my staff and making a spectacle of yourself in front of numerous guests. Such egotism has no place in my hotel."

"And such open hostility by your staff should have no place in your hotel either. The Fairweathers specifically asked for a ground-floor room — "

"And the Fairweathers were allocated the kind of room indicated on Ultimate Tours' booking form," he cut in, his voice darkly angry. "If you'd been a little more vigilant yourself, Miss Hamilton, you would have noticed that a mistake had been made back in London, probably by some dizzy, half-witted inexperienced clerk."

Juliet's moment of triumph was shattered. Could that be right? Could there have been a mistake on the booking form? Her skin flamed and the blood rushed to her sore head until she felt it might burst.

"I'd like to see the booking form," she said, unable to quell the tremor in her voice.

"Of course. I would expect you to. I'll notify reception to find it. In the meantime — "

"Now!" she demanded. "I'd like to see it now, please."

His teeth pressed together, giving new strength to the line of his jaw. "Very well. Come with me."

He swung round and strode off down the carpeted corridor. Juliet had to half run to keep up with him. She suspected she was going to her doom and was hardly aware of the greetings and smiles bestowed on her by guests.

At the desk in the large and spacious foyer the receptionists immediately acted upon Reece Carter's terse request, taking only a few moments to produce the form in question.

He took it from the young woman and ran a quick glance over it, then handed it to Juliet. Carefully she skimmed the badly-spelled computer print-out. The relevant information stared her back in the face, confirming her worst fears. The Fairweathers might have requested a ground-floor room but the tour clerk back in London had omitted to stipulate this. Juliet could have wrung the clerk's neck.

"You're quite right," she conceded, swallowing her pride. "There has been a mistake."

Her admission flowed over him. "The guests here," he told her loftily, "are the kind of people who think nothing of paying 2,000 pounds sterling per week to stay at this hotel." He ran a superior and arrogant eye over her and his tone was dark with sarcasm. "That may be hard for you to grasp, Miss Hamilton, coming from Spain. I won't have the reputation of my hotel sullied by an over-zealous tour representative. Much as I dislike doing so, your attitude and behaviour will be closely monitored from now on."

Brusquely he moved away leaving

her standing holding her briefcase in front of her like a schoolgirl who had been severely reprimanded by the headmaster.

She had wanted to show this man flushed with self-importance that, though young and inexperienced, she was still capable of acting out her role as representative of one of the world's leading tour operators. She had wanted to be superior, too; she had wanted him to recognize her influential position. But he had slapped her down and she had ended up coming away from the confrontation smarting.

Everyone seemed to be watching her. The two receptionists whispered between themselves and flung surreptitious glances in her direction; hotel guests, curious about the unusual exchange they had just witnessed, diplomatically avoided her eyes, and a waiter who had stood at the entrance to the restaurant moved away quickly when she looked across at him. It was obvious that news of the disagreement would be common knowledge within the hour.

Tears of hurt and frustration welled up in her, but too proud to let anyone see them she hurried back to her bungalow and gave vent to them in solitude.

3

"OH, would you believe it!" groaned Alison Gregory. "This big expanse of gorgeous beach and not a young, hunky man in sight!" Her striped dress billowed in the stiff breeze and she shaded her eyes from the sun with her hand as she made a thorough study of the pink-tinged sands.

Alison was on duty that day, dividing her time between the Island Cove Hotel and the Coral Reef Hotel just further along the coast. Juliet had the afternoon off because she was on airport transfer duty that night which meant very little sleep, and none at all if the plane was late.

At eleven that evening she was due to accompany a group of guests whose holiday had ended to the airport. The replacement holidaymakers weren't due in until one in the morning, which meant clicking her heels and going over her checklist in the airport lounge whilst waiting for their arrival.

It was the downside of an otherwise interesting job, and was usually undertaken in the dead of night for air companies seemed to have a predilection for arriving at the most inconvenient hour.

"It's the same every year," Alison complained, sitting down beside Juliet on the warm sand and taking a few minutes out from dealing with people's queries. "And I've been in Bermuda for three years. Hordes of men, but they're either too old or on their honeymoon. Would you believe it? Thirty years old and not even a proposal. Where are all the masculine hunks shown in the tour brochures? That's what I want to know."

Juliet smiled and traced a pattern in the sand between her feet with her finger. "Probably shivering in England dreaming about the modelling job they did in Bermuda for a few days last year. There's always Jan Peters."

Alison made a face. "He's all right, I suppose. A bit too young for me. Anyway I'd have to show a liking for sport and I'm a strong believer that women have no need to be sporty. I have enough exercise running around after this lot." And she nodded in the direction of the near-naked bodies stretched out in rows like a mass barbecue, and sizzling in expensive sun oil. She glanced across at Juliet and took off her sunglasses. "You don't seem to be bubbling with vitality today. How's everything going?"

"Oh, all right, I suppose." Juliet leaned back on her elbows, stretched out her legs and studied the sea, avoiding Alison's gaze. "I crossed swords with Mr Carter the other day."

"As in Reece Carter?" Alison sounded surprised. "Bermuda's very own eligible bachelor? Good Lord, what happened?"

"He thinks I'm too young for the job and too inexperienced, so he's put me on trial."

"On trial? You're having me on!"

"I'm not." She brushed some sand from her jade-coloured shorts. "He even came into my welcoming reception and stood at the back, watching. I nearly died. I had such a whopper of a headache, too."

"He doesn't usually involve himself with the day to day running of the hotel. Alan Scarlet deals with that side. What did you say to him?"

"I virtually told him to keep off my back as I wasn't employed by him. I also told him I wasn't impressed with his staff."

"Ouch!" Alison grimaced. "What did he say to that?"

"You don't want to know, Alison."

"Holy Moses! You must have really rubbed him up the wrong way. Not such a good start, eh?"

Juliet groaned and fell back, lying flat on the warm sand. "Not you, too! Alan

Scarlet said the same thing."

"About you being absent when the guests arrived?"

"Mmm. I don't know whether I'm going to like it here. Everybody's so distant and unfriendly. Alan Scarlet makes my skin creep, and Reece Carter — well, I can't stand the sight of him. At least in Spain I had friends."

Which was all quite true. Juliet, along with three other reps, had rented a house in the resort and had a marvellous time. But she was in a totally different world now — a world of sub-tropical beauty, of flamboyant wealth and select hotels, and proprietors who thought they ruled the world.

"You've only been here five minutes!" Alison reasoned. "And I'm your friend, Jan's your friend. What else do you want?"

"I don't know what I would have done without you," Juliet confided. "You've been marvellous." She rolled over onto her side, facing Alison, and propped her head in her hand. "I've been wondering whether to put in for a transfer."

"So soon? I wouldn't if I were you. Not unless you want to go back to sunny Spain. Being posted to Bermuda is not just one step up the ladder, Juliet. It's a giant leap. They don't usually do that for trainees just out of nappies. And anyway, out here you might just net yourself a rich husband."

Juliet laughed despite her despondency. "As you said, they've all been netted. And those that haven't are not up my street."

At that point a particularly large, overweight and deeply bronzed man in brightly coloured Bermuda shorts ambled across the sand and came to stand beside them. American was stamped all over him and he positively oozed wealth. He smiled down at them and, in a very forthright way, ogled Juliet's slim, brown legs stretched out on the sand.

"Yes, I can see what you mean," murmured Alison, getting to her feet and brushing the sand from her dress. "Well, duty calls," she said out loud, and with a polite smile at the elderly man she took her leave.

Left alone Juliet also sprang to her feet, offered the American an equally polite smile that she hoped he would not interpret as a sign of encouragement, and made her escape along the beach.

She hadn't thought about which direction to take, so eager had she been to escape the intentions of the American; and once she had established that he was not following her she settled down to assess her surroundings.

Just ahead was a small marina with a jetty and a variety of boats moored in the bay. At the far side of the jetty, rising and falling gently with each wave and enjoying its own exclusive mooring was a sleek, high-performance powerboat in gleaming red. Juliet gazed at it in wonderment.

"That one's not for hire, missy."

She spun round. A heavily-built,

beaming Negro emerged from a hut and came down the beach towards her. He wore khaki-coloured shorts, a white T-shirt that struggled to cover him, and had flip-flops on his huge feet.

"I didn't think it was," she smiled back.

"She's called *Razzmatazz* and belongs to Mr Carter up at the hotel," he informed her. "He brought it over from Florida in the spring."

"I probably couldn't afford to hire it anyway," she laughed. "It is beautiful, though, isn't it?"

"Yes, she sure is a little firecracker. Fifty foot long and can reach seventy miles an hour. She's all fitted out inside, too. Sheer luxury in motion."

"How much is it to hire one of the smaller boats?"

"What kind were you thinking of, missy?"

"Oh, nothing too complicated. Maybe one of the motor-boats."

"Those are twelve dollars an hour."

Juliet's face fell. "I've only got a ten

53

dollar note with me."

A silence followed as both the boatman and Juliet shifted in indecision. Then a different voice, a voice she recognized above all others, and one that made her stiffen, intervened.

"That's no problem. Ten dollars will suffice, Joshua. Pull one in."

"Yes, sir, Mr Carter." The boatman ambled down to the water's edge whilst Juliet turned to face Reece Carter.

Dressed in white shorts, a T-shirt which matched the colour of his boat exactly, and a navy blue cotton sweater draped around his shoulders and tied loosely at the front, Reece Carter stepped from one of the many paths leading back up to the hotel, and onto the warm sand. Juliet couldn't help noticing his slim, athletic frame and muscular limbs, bronzed by the sun.

"I prefer to pay the full amount," she retorted. "I'll go back to the bungalow for another two dollars."

"Nonsense. I won't hear of it." His mouth quirked wryly. "I'm sure the hotel isn't going to miss two dollars."

He thrust both hands into the pockets of his shorts and let his gaze stray away from her. His relaxed attitude seemed to suggest he had forgotten about the row they had had a few days earlier. Juliet hadn't forgotten, though, and remained distant and wary.

For the next few moments they both watched as Joshua hauled a small, unassuming motor-boat into the shallower water. Then Reece turned back to her, running a derisive glance over her face.

"Think you can handle this little gem?"

His voice rang with sarcasm and Juliet felt a strong urge to hit him. "Mr Carter, it might surprise you to learn that we have them in England. On boating lakes in parks."

"Boating lakes in parks, though, are not the same as the sea. And what's more the wind is fresh today. There are small breakers out there."

"I've no intention of making my

way to mainland America. I really can manage, thank you."

Turning her back on him she offered the patiently waiting Joshua the ten dollar note then climbed aboard the small motor-boat. Joshua bent down to untie the rope that moored it to the beach.

"Wait a minute, Joshua . . . " Reece strode down the shelving beach, took off his navy blue canvas deck shoes, and without invitation splashed through the ankle-deep water and stepped into the boat, installing himself comfortably next to Juliet. "Just a precautionary measure," he said breezily. "And if you really are an expert at handling one of these things on a choppy sea, well then, we've nothing to worry about, have we?"

Juliet stared at him in open-mouthed shock. She was so furious at his high-handed manner in inviting himself to join her that she could find nothing to say in return. Her first thought was to climb right back out of the boat and storm back up the beach, but Joshua had already pushed it out and pride and dignity prevented her from making a fool of herself. Instead she made a show of moving as far away from him as possible so that she did not come into physical contact with him at all.

Jamming her foot flat on the accelerator pedal the small boat lurched forward into the deeper water, flinging Reece back against the wooden back rest of the seat then throwing him forwards again.

"You won't get much more than about ten miles an hour out of her," he told her wryly. "She's built for a sedate sail around the cove."

"So, I'm also being supervised in my off-duty hours, am I?" she commented pointedly.

"Not supervised, Miss Hamilton. Accompanied," he retorted.

Juliet took no notice and recklessly steered the motor boat on, aiming head-on at each breaker in order to give him the most uncomfortable ride.

"If you hit a wave the wrong way," he warned, "we could both be thrown overboard."

"Then I hope you know how to swim," she retorted dryly. "I didn't bargain on doing any life-saving, today."

The laughing amusement in his eyes reached out to stoke up Juliet's simmering anger. He leaned back in the seat, stretched out his long legs and lifted his face to the sun. He even ran his arm along the back rest behind her, as if he were thoroughly enjoying the uncomfortable sail. Juliet felt like screaming with frustration, for there was no way in this under-powered little boat that she could jolt him out of his complacency.

Farther out in the cove the sea was incredibly clear, and she could see right down to the seabed with its rippled sand, reefs of coral and brightly coloured fish wafting between the green plankton.

Reece suggested she slow down, and without invitation he began to tell her something of the sea creatures that inhabited the warm waters, pointing out and naming the various fish that darted away from the hull of the boat. At times, in his apparent eagerness to indicate some interesting detail, he leaned right across her, causing his warm, brown thigh to brush against her own.

Juliet attempted to ignore his closeness and tried to appear indifferent to his comments, but he was just too good a teacher to ignore. In only half an hour she had learned more about the seabed than she had in her lifetime.

"There are a number of rocks close by which lie only just below the surface," he warned her. "Do you want me to take the wheel?"

"No, thank you." She turned the wheel in order to steer the boat back to shore. "I rented the boat. I'd like my ten dollars worth. And I really can manage."

"Such independence!" he murmured, as ever nonchalant, and stretched himself out once more, arms folded across his chest, eyes closed, face turned up to the sun.

A shadow, just beneath the surface of the water, glided some way in front of the boat. Juliet decelerated and screwed up her eyes against the blinding sparkle from the sea in order to identify it. Then in the next instant the surface broke and a dark form reared up just yards from the bow, wearing snorkel and mask. Juliet's reaction was quick and only natural, but it also turned out to be rather unfortunate.

In order to avoid running the snorkeler down she spun the wheel of the motor-boat. It immediately responded to her actions, veering off sharply to the left. Had Reece not been off guard, he might have stayed dry, but because his body was in a relaxed state he didn't stand a chance. He just tipped over the side — like one might fall out of bed — and entered the sea cleanly and neatly.

Horrified, Juliet snatched her foot

from the pedal, brought the boat back to its former position and scanned the immediate area. There was no sign of either Reece nor the snorkeler. A sense of panic began to rise in her as her eyes raked the spume the boat had recently churned up. Had she run down the snorkeler? And where was Reece Carter?

She stood up and clambered onto the seat, leaning her hands on the stern of the boat and peering down at the rudder, but there was no sign of either of the men in the abating sea.

Then the boat dipped suddenly at the front, and spinning round she saw Reece, both arms resting on the bow, an accusing gaze fixed on her. His dark hair, soaked with seawater, was flattened against his head, and beads of water streamed down his tanned face.

Flicking his dripping hair back from his forehead, he let go of the bow and swam round the side. The boat pitched crazily as he levered himself up. Juliet had to move quickly and sit on the other side to prevent it from overturning. In one smooth, fluid movement Reece climbed back into the boat and sat down beside her.

"Such aggression, too!" he commented quietly, taking the sweater from around his shoulders and wringing it out over the side.

For long moments they stared at each other in expectant silence. Held prisoner by his sombre, unwavering gaze she felt around with her right hand, found what she was looking for and handed him his dry deck shoes. It was a gesture that didn't break the tense atmosphere entirely but it was enough to pass as an olive branch. Juliet could see the funny side of it and wanted to laugh; but he still looked rather too forbidding, so she fought down the giggle rising in her.

Dragging her eyes from his she stared down guiltily at the water that streamed from him to form a pool in the hull of the boat. Just saying 'I'm sorry', seemed so inadequate.

"Memo to myself," he murmured. "Reece, consider yourself good and truly reprimanded for forcing yourself on Miss Hamilton."

In normal circumstances his use of this suggestive undertone would have been recognized by Juliet for what it was — an acceptance of the olive branch she had offered him. But she was horrified to think he believed her capable of such a drastic show of resentment.

"You don't think I did that on purpose, do you?" Her fingers were pressed to her breastbone, emphasizing her words.

"I would like to think not. But I can't see any other reason."

Juliet's mouth dropped open. "There was a snorkeler. He just bobbed up in front of me. I had to swerve to avoid him."

"I didn't see him."

"But of course you didn't. You had your eyes closed."

"And anyway snorkelers and divers

63

aren't allowed in this area of the bay,"
he put in.

Juliet paused, now, her mind fighting
to present the facts exactly as they had
happened. "I saw a shadow up ahead. I
slowed down. Then this man just broke
the surface only yards in front. He had
a mask on and a snorkel."

Reece scanned the empty sea around
them, then offered her an indulgent
smile. "Where is he now?"

"How should I know? He disappeared
at the same time you did. I didn't
watch where he went. I was more
worried about . . . " She stopped and
looked away, avoiding his shrewd gaze.
"What happened to you anyway? Why
did you take so long to surface?"

Now a slight curve could be perceived
at one corner of his mouth. "Were you
worried?"

"Well, of course I . . . " She
stopped abruptly, seeing the laughing
amusement in his eyes. "Of course
I wasn't," she snapped back, angry
that he should be reading her so

64

clearly. "I'm sure you can look after yourself."

Slithering round on the wet seat she faced the bow and put her foot on the pedal, hardly seeing the approaching beach for the conflicting feelings rioting within her.

A young woman was standing on the beach, tall, long-legged and evenly tanned, with golden blonde hair blowing in the breeze. Beside Juliet, Reece suddenly stirred and waved, hardly waiting for Joshua to tether the boat before striding over the side.

"Reece!" the woman called. "What are you doing in that old thing?"

"Taking a dip!" he called back, indicating his dripping clothes.

"God, what happened to you?"

He glanced down at himself, his eyes taking in his dishevelled state. "Miss Hamilton decided she wanted to pay me back, and ditched me overboard."

"Pay you back?" the woman queried playfully. "What for?"

"I'm not quite sure." Reece's dark

eyebrows shot up and he turned back to Juliet. She felt the intensity of his gaze as his grey eyes searched deep into her face. "What exactly did I do to deserve a dipping?"

Juliet shrugged and looked away. He was playing with her emotions and she detested him for it. "I need to get changed," Reece announced. "Hang on a minute, will you, Koelle, whilst I run up to the hotel."

"I'll come with you," she said, moving like a graceful gazelle to the water's edge but taking great care not to get herself wet. "You obviously need an eye keeping on you." And she laughed, a deep, seductive laugh from the depths of her throat.

Reece turned back to Juliet. "Thank you for the ride, Miss Hamilton. It was . . . different. But you won't be offended, will you, if I don't accompany you again?"

Juliet laughed shortly. "On the contrary, I should be delighted."

His mouth quirked at one corner,

then flinging his screwed up sweater over one shoulder he splashed through the shallow water towards the waiting girl.

"Mr Carter," Juliet called out on impulse, and he spared her a quick glance; "I'm sorry."

"No matter, Miss Hamilton," he declaimed with a dismissive wave of his hand. "I was going to take a bath anyway."

4

JULIET stepped out of the boat into the warm, shallow water and studied the wet patches on her shorts.

"I guess it was a little bit rough out there, missy," Joshua observed wryly.

She glanced up into the full-moon face of the black man, noting the flash of his white teeth as he gave her an oblique smile.

"Choppy, Joshua," she amended.

"I'm surprised Mr Carter ended up in the water. He's an expert sailor. In fact, now Miss Wiseman's here, he'll be taking *Razzmatazz* out. He likes to go out whenever he can and take the boat for a spin around the bay. If you hang around you'll see her leave. Once he touches the deeper water, just at the end of the pier, Mr Carter always hits the throttle. Then her nose lifts, and man, does she go. It's worth watching."

Juliet thought it was a thrill she could well forego and made an excuse about getting into some dry clothes. But by the time she had ambled across the beach to where the coconut matting umbrellas were dotted around, the roar of an engine brought her head round, and she was in time to see the gleaming red powerboat emerge from the far side of the jetty. At the wheel stood Reece Carter, freshly-clothed and wearing sunglasses now, and by his side the willowy and leggy Koelle Wiseman, poised in readiness for the imminent force of wind that would sweep over them.

With another rather ostentatious roar *Razzmatazz* thrust herself forward, raising her bows to almost forty-five degrees as she arched around the end of the jetty in a cloud of white spume and spray. Within seconds she was out into the bay, skimming the waves and leaving a pale green wake behind her.

A long, low whistle at her left shoulder brought her head round and she saw Jan Peters by her side, arms akimbo as he followed the disappearing boat. His face was almost green with envy.

"Wow!" he breathed. "What a little firecracker! Will you watch her go!"

"A showy display of exhibitionism!" she retorted.

Jan dragged his eyes away from the red speck out in the bay and looked her over curiously. "My word, it hasn't taken you long, has it?"

"What for?"

"To realize that everyone here has to prove they're richer than their neighbour."

Juliet shrugged. "There are many wealthy people here. I don't begrudge them that wealth."

"But it's immoral, isn't it, that some folk can afford to pay out a million dollars for a boat like that?"

"If that is what Reece Carter wants to spend his money on, then good luck to him. If you had a million dollars, what would you spend it on?"

70

A wicked smile crept over his face. "Probably a boat like that."

"There you are!" Juliet laughed with him. "You're only envious!"

"Of course! Aren't you? Wouldn't you like to be in that boat with him?"

Juliet's toes curled inside her canvas shoes. "I've just been in a boat with him. It was an experience that neither of us is in a hurry to relive."

Jan shot her a sideways glance. "I heard about your little disagreement with him."

"Word does travel fast. When I think back over what happened I can't help shuddering. It's a wonder I'm not on the plane back to London."

"I doubt he'd do that. Reece Carter considers himself a good judge of character. If he had really thought you were a troublemaker you'd have been out on your backside within minutes. So cheer up! Listen, I'm due to give a tennis lesson in five minutes so I can't stop. Mrs Andrina Saville. Have you come across her yet?"

71

Juliet shook her head.

"What a treat is in store for you! Sixty-five, a widow, loaded and spoiled rotten. Do you fancy coming scuba-diving sometime?"

"I'd love to but . . . well, it's just that . . . "

"You can swim, can't you?"

"Oh, yes, quite well. It's just that I've never dived under water."

"That's no problem. I'll teach you."

"You must have loads of pupils demanding your attention . . . "

"I can find a place for an English siren. When are you free?"

"Probably when you're not."

"I'll teach you in my spare time."

"But that's not fair on you. Your free time must be sacred."

"That's true, but most of it is spent underwater anyway. I like diving to the hundreds of wrecks around the islands. Let's think . . . how about Saturday morning?"

Juliet thought it over. "That's fine by me."

"We'll meet at the pool at 7 a.m. before it gets busy. Don't eat anything beforehand. Now I must go or Mrs Andrina Saville will get impatient. She fancies me like mad, you know."

With a grin he left Juliet and she watched him run effortlessly across the beach. He wasn't very tall, but he was perfectly proportioned for his size, and very agile. She noticed that greetings from all corners of the beach were bestowed on him by women who were obviously his pupils in one sport or another.

As she made her way through the hot, humid gardens and into the area of the swimming pool she heard her name being called. Her glance fell on a shaded corner where Mr and Mrs Fairweather were sitting at a table enjoying their morning coffee under a yellow and white striped umbrella. Another couple, whom Juliet did not recognize, sat with them.

Mrs Fairweather smiled and beckoned her over.

"Come and join us . . . Archie, there's a chair behind you. Nobody's using it. Pull it around for Juliet." She glanced about the gardens. "Where's the waiter? I'll ask him to bring another cup and saucer."

"No, don't bother, Mrs Fairweather. I can't stop long. I have to change," Juliet said, pointing to her wet shorts and sitting down in the chair Archie placed behind her.

"Been paddling, dear?" Mrs Fairweather queried.

"No, I've been out in a small motor-boat."

"I didn't think it looked that rough out there," Mrs Fairweather observed.

"It's not. My steering wasn't too good."

"Ah, I see. Juliet, this is Mr and Mrs Carter. Reece's parents. Jenny, Colin, this is the rep for Ultimate Tours I was telling you about."

"Hello, Miss Hamilton," said Jenny Carter. "Susan has been so grateful for your help. With Archie in a wheelchair it's much better to have a room on the ground floor."

Juliet returned her smile, suddenly realizing that the woman sitting across from her was an older version of the one done in oils and hanging in Reece Carter's office. Her beauty was still strongly in evidence and her serenity seemed to envelop her like a halo. Juliet wondered how such a calm, sweet-natured woman could have borne a son as aggressive as Reece Carter.

"It's what I'm here for," Juliet said modestly. "Are you comfortable in your new room, Mrs Fairweather?"

"Entirely, dear. It has a lovely view over the gardens. It couldn't be better."

"It's not often a mix-up of that sort occurs," said Colin Carter.

At sixty-three Reece's father was still virile and handsome. He wasn't quite as tall as his son, but the likeness was unmistakable — the same dark hair, good bone structure, alert, shrewd grey eyes and a deep baritone voice which all combined to give him an aura of power and style. It gave Juliet an insight into how Reece might look in thirty years time. Not an unpleasant insight, either.

"No doubt Reece will get to the bottom of it," Colin was saying.

Juliet shifted uncomfortably and smiled weakly. She wasn't going to get herself involved on that score. Let Reece Carter explain to his father what had happened and that it was the fault of Ultimate Tours.

"I've just watched him sail off in *Razzmatazz*," Juliet informed them.

"Oh, that flirty thing!" Jenny muttered in a half disapproving way. "He got her in the spring and he's been like a little boy with a new toy ever since."

"What's that dear?" queried Susan Fairweather.

"Reece has got himself a new mistress," Colin announced drolly.

"Eh?" questioned Archie, eyebrows raising in delight.

"A boat," Jenny amended, flinging a reproving glance at her husband.

"It's the same thing," Colin said dismissively. "He can't leave it alone."

"Has he sold the old one, then?" asked Archie.

"To an American couple in Florida. The Wisemans. Their daughter, Koelle, is the Exotica rep in Bermuda. You'll know who I mean, Archie — tall, leggy blonde bit, never wears the top half of her bikini on the beach . . . "

"Ah, yes, I know . . . " Archie nodded with a knowing grin.

"Now, now, you two," Jenny intervened with a frown of mock disapproval. "You'll bring on your blood pressure."

"Just teasing!" Colin leaned across and gave his wife's hand a loving squeeze. "Well, anyway," he went on, "Reece wanted something with a bit more get up and go. So he sailed the old one over last year and came back with this one. It's called *Razzmatazz* and is the last word in luxury."

From there Colin described it for the interested Fairweathers, explaining about the length, height, fuel capacity, draft and weight, which led on to great technical detail such as engine, batteries, bilges and fuel filters. Juliet wasn't too interested, and neither, it seemed, was Jenny Carter for she turned away from the men and engaged Juliet in conversation.

"When did you arrive, Miss Hamilton?"

"Four days ago. I've replaced Jane Tyson who's been transferred to Hawaii."

"How nice for her. I think she wanted a change. Have you settled in?"

"More or less," she replied lightly, thinking that if it wasn't for Jenny's son she would have settled in even faster. The presence of Reece Carter was the only thing she really objected to on the island, and he was an occupational hazard consistent with working within a small, elite community. "I'm off duty at the moment because I'm on airport transfer tonight."

"Does that mean little sleep?"

"I'm afraid so."

Jenny made a sympathetic face then said, "The hotel has had connections with Ultimate Tours as far back as I can remember. How long do you reckon Colin?"

"What, darling?" Her husband interrupted his description of Reece's new boat.

"Ultimate Tours. When did they first start sending their clients to us?"

"Well," he demurred, puffing out his cheeks in thought, "I remember them sending reps here way back in the fifties. We have a very special rapport with the company."

Juliet swallowed, horrified to think how very close she had come to being instrumental in severing those ties.

"Because of that I always like to keep in contact with the Ultimate girls," Jenny was saying. "Will you come to a little aperitifs party we're having on Saturday lunchtime? Alison will be there."

And your son? she wanted to ask.

Will your son be there? She wished she could refuse the invitation, but she was representing her company. It was her job to socialize on behalf of Ultimate Tours and help maintain those ties cemented before she was born and of which Colin Carter was so proud.

"You're very kind, Mrs Carter. Thank you. What time?"

"Oh, around 11.30. I think that was the time I told Alison. There'll just be a few people — my daughter and her husband will be there and one or two other hoteliers from the island. There's no need to dress. Anything informal. We don't stand on ceremony, do we, Colin?"

"You won't get me in a collar and tie job at Saturday lunchtime."

Jenny patted his arm. "I know, dear. Trying to get you into a collar and tie at *any* time is a work of art."

Juliet smiled and leaned back in her chair, relaxed in their company and comforted by the intimate banter between Reece's parents. Such gentleness towards each other, thoughtfulness, humour, and friendship, too. It reminded her of home and her own parents. An amiable, down-to-earth couple. Pity their son was not made from the same mould.

Late that evening Juliet gathered the handful of guests from the Island Cove Hotel and those from the Coral Reef and accompanied them to the old-fashioned white two-storeyed building that served as the Civil Air Terminal. Having supervised the unloading of their luggage from the minibus she directed them to the check-in desks where she said goodbye and wished them all a safe journey.

Two hours of waiting were now in front of her until the next plane load arrived. She yawned, stretched, then wandered around the deserted airport for a time, studying the semi-tropical plants that brightened the area. Finally, feeling at a low ebb, she went in search of a drinks machine. The coffee was quite good even though it was dispensed in a plastic cup, and choosing a seat in one corner of the almost deserted arrivals hall she sat down to wait.

She was looking over the list of the incoming holidaymakers when she became aware of another person in the hall. An indifferent glance revealed the American girl, Koelle Wiseman, standing at the drinks dispenser.

The girl saw her, smiled and ambled over to her. Aged around the mid twenties she made even the obligatory uniform of Exotica reps — pleated cream skirt and navy jacket — look elegant. Juliet could not deny she was attractive with her tall, slim figure, and her long blonde hair tied back in a neat pony tail that swung from side to side as she walked.

"Hi!" The girl dumped her briefcase on the floor and scanned the empty hall. "Isn't this a godawful time to be hanging around an airport?"

Juliet nodded and smiled. "I could think of better places to be."

Koelle sat down in the seat next to Juliet and crossed one long leg over the other. "I nearly didn't make it. I had this really heavy date! I mean we're talking delicious — young, handsome . . . and rich. I had to leave halfway through dinner to come here. He sure wasn't so pleased."

Juliet looked away, wondering if the date she referred to was Reece Carter, and just how heavy their relationship was.

"I'm the Exotica rep, by the way. I've got five coming in for the Coral Reef and Island Cove. What about you?"

"Ultimate Tours. Eight adults, three children. Same hotels."

Koelle groaned. "Honestly, what organization!" She sighed with a skywards roll of her big, brown eyes. "They could have fitted them all on one minibus then only one rep would have been needed."

Juliet nodded, seeing the practicability in this.

"Say," Koelle said, as if suddenly realizing what a good idea it was, "you couldn't do me a favour, could you?"

Juliet shot her a sideways glance, her look questioning and wary. "What is it?"

"Could you pick up my lot and bring them over with yours? Give them the usual welcoming spiel."

"What about your minibus?"

"Oh, no problem. I'll cancel it right away. All the passengers would fit in one bus. If you could just see them to their hotels I'd be so grateful. I'd really like to get back to my date."

Juliet shifted uncomfortably, detesting being put on the spot like this. "I don't think that's such a good idea," she said. Somehow those big, brown eyes were making her feel like a spoilsport. "Not so much for me," she put in quickly, "but for you. If Exotica got to find out . . ."

"Yeah, you're right, I guess. I could be up you-know-what creek." She placed her pink lips over the rim of the plastic cup, took a sip and shuddered. "Jeez, what awful coffee! Doesn't anyone know how to make decent coffee around here?" She placed the full cup back on the table in front of her then glanced across at Juliet.

"I'm Koelle Wiseman, by the way."

"Juliet Hamilton."

"Hamilton." Now a slight perceptible change came into the air. Koelle's eyes narrowed as she gave Juliet a long, searching look. "You aren't the girl who Reece was with when he fell in the sea earlier today?"

"Yes, that was me." A hot flush crept over Juliet. She averted her eyes and gave her attention to the list of arriving passengers on her clipboard. For something to do she began to count the names again. "I always hate this bit, ticking off the names as they arrive. I'm dreading the day that someone's name is not on the list."

"It happened to me once." Koelle opened her handbag and searched around, bringing out a cigarette which she lit at leisure. "A couple of old biddies bound for the Island Cove. I hadn't a clue what to do and they were getting pretty irate. So I bundled them into the bus and took them to the hotel. Reece was ever so good about it. Took the burden right off my shoulders. He fixed up the poor dears with a room and told me not to worry about it. He'd sort it out with Exotica. Why were you out sailing with him?"

The intonation of her voice, though light, was touched with a suspicion that went farther than light interest.

Juliet kept her eyes fixed on the list of names attached to her clipboard, and answered airily. "Oh, he wasn't so sure it was safe for me out in the bay alone in such a small boat. The wind was fresh and the sea choppy."

"Choppy enough for him to end up in it?" Her voice held a hint of incredulity. "Reece didn't exactly say why you pitched him overboard."

It was a prompting statement, and the silence that followed was an indication that Koelle expected her to expand. A distant roar of heavy engines broke the stillness. Juliet glanced at her watch, blessing the early arrival of the plane from England.

"My plane's arriving," she said, gathering her things and standing up. Peering out of the windows she could make out the winking lights of the plane as it descended towards the runway.

"You haven't been here in Bermuda that long, have you?" Koelle questioned.

"About a week."

"I thought so. Then you won't be familiar with the rules. One, it's not good form for reps to socialize with employees of the hotel. And two, especially not the proprietor."

Juliet was still watching the plane as it completed its touchdown with squeals, thuds and bounces, but turned back quickly and gave the American girl an accusing glance.

Seeing it the girl tilted her chin in defiance. "It's different for me," she explained loftily. "I'm not just a rep.

Reece is a family friend."

"Then you have my sympathies," Juliet quipped back and turned away, hardly able to believe such childish, self-assurance in a grown woman.

She walked towards the arrivals desk but she was trembling. Koelle's bumptious comment was clearly a warning and her skin flamed hot at the American girl's lofty attitude. Determinedly she pushed away her irritation and welcomed the small group of English tourists. Koelle had vanished from the arrivals hall when Juliet led her guests through to the waiting minibus.

5

JULIET set her alarm clock for 6.30, wanting to come round at leisure and be in plenty of time for her first underwater diving lesson. Getting up early had never really bothered her for she was not a night-owl and preferred to go to bed early and read a good book.

It being so early in the morning there was not a soul in sight when she padded quietly through the gardens to the swimming pool. Out at sea, on the horizon, a thick bank of billowing cloud was forming; but inland the tropical sun continued to shine, ricocheting off the ripples in the pool. The movement of the water suggested that someone had been in before her, swimming in the sun-warmed water.

It was almost certainly Jan, although there was no sign of him. Then as she walked along the side of the sparkling blue water she glimpsed a man, leaning both arms on the waist-high wall that surrounded the pool area and gazing out across the gardens to the dawn-reflecting sea.

Because the sun was in her eyes and obscuring her vision she thought it was Jan and began to slip off her baggy T-shirt. But as she was about to pull it over her head the man turned round and she found her gaze resting on Reece Carter. He had picked up a towel and was drying himself off. If he saw her he did not come near, neither did he wave or make any sign of acknowledgment. She continued to take off her T-shirt, dropped it on one of the sun-chairs behind her, then bent down and slithered noiselessly into the warm water.

For a while she trod water, watching from the corner of her eye as he rough-towelled his dark hair, then she set off and swam two leisurely lengths of the pool. Afterwards she heaved herself out of the water, strong, slender arms holding her weight with little difficulty. As she stood up and squeezed the water from her thick, chestnut hair he came towards her and for an instant or two his eyes took in all the smooth lines and sensuous curves revealed by her one-piece costume.

It was a daring little swimsuit in a bright yellow and white spotted material that she had bought on impulse only last month. The only drawback was that when it was wet it became like a second skin, clinging and moulding itself to every line of her body.

She reached for her towel and began to rub her hair, allowing the majority of the towel to fall down in front of her. She hadn't missed the way his eyes travelled over the upthrust of her breasts, the curve of her hips, and the contour of her slender thighs. In that look she saw the recognition of her as a woman. She was shaken by the sensation, and her skin crawled with a sudden heat.

"Up bright and early this morning," he commented.

"I'm not one for lying in bed. I woke early and decided to have a swim before the crowds gathered."

"Me too. I always take a dip about this time in the morning," he told her and Juliet surprised herself by slotting it neatly into her memory for future reference.

An old Negro carrying a hoe over his shoulder emerged from the semi-tropical gardens and shuffled across the terrace, returning Reece's greeting with a friendly one of his own. He adjusted the old straw sunhat on his head then took up the hoe and began to rake and weed between the hibiscus and oleander bushes. It was not easy for his frail frame, and as he went to tug at a particularly stubborn weed, he stumbled and half fell. Concerned Juliet moved to offer him help, but Reece gripped her wrist.

"No, don't do that. Just leave him."

"What?" The command in his voice

brought her head round sharply.

"Leave him." His tone was clear and strong.

She stared up at him for a stunned instant then shook his hand from her wrist. "My God, so it still goes on."

Reece flicked his eyes from the old gardener who was on his feet again, and frowned. "What does?"

Juliet slowly shook her head, immersed in her own incredulity. "Black, white. Slave, master. No wonder your hotel is immaculate."

Confusion clouded his eyes. "Slaves? What are you talking about?"

"I'm talking about that man. He's too old to be doing that kind of work."

The light dawned. "Ah, I see," he retorted dryly. "So you think I'm the cruel master, and Luke's the poor slave." Reece uttered a short, unamused grunt and bestowed a disdainful glance on her. "Slavery went out with the Ark, Miss Hamilton. Luke used to be a gardener here until he retired ten years ago. The gardens of the hotel have always been his life. We have a verbal agreement. He comes here whenever he feels like it, and in return I give him a chicken, eggs, milk, whatever he needs."

Reece turned away from her, his eyes coming to rest, not without affection, on the old man now bending to tug at a stubborn weed.

"He's a proud man, Miss Hamilton. If you went to help him it would embarrass him deeply. He would think that perhaps I considered him finished, too old, senile. Many of the hoteliers do the same for their old employees. In a way they're setting themselves up as their guardians."

"Oh." Juliet felt embarrassed at her rash conclusion. "It's a kind gesture," she said.

Reece spun back round, his eyes suddenly flashing like steel in the sun.

"Kind?" It was bordering on a shout, and there was a hint of mockery at her choice of word. Juliet moved back in alarm. "Whatever the other hoteliers are doing I'm not doing it out of kindness," he went on, "but because I value the time and trouble Luke and his like have given to the hotel. He has worked his fingers to the bone in these gardens since as far back as I can remember. I would never give him a golden handshake then turn my back on him. If you can't understand that — " He clamped his mouth shut and with an effort remained silent. After a moment he said, "Have you eaten yet?"

"No." Despite an effort Juliet heard her voice shaking.

"Will you have breakfast with me?"

Juliet trembled and coloured. Then anger overtook her alarm. How dare he berate her so harshly in one breath then invite her to have breakfast with him in the next? What kind of a man was he?

"I eat very little breakfast, thank you. Usually just orange juice and maybe a slice of toast."

"Then that's what we'll have," he said.

"No, thank you." Her voice began to tremble. She bent down and picked up her T-shirt. "I really don't want anything. If you'll excuse me I'll go back to my bungalow."

Only in the solitude of her quarters did her anger and alarm begin to abate. She was glad because she didn't want Jan to see her so agitated and confused. Why had she reacted so harshly to Reece, and why was it that whatever she said seemed to make him angry?

Apart from old Luke they had been completely alone in a beautiful setting with the sun shining, the pool glittering and the heady scent of the tropical flowers. They should have been relaxed, friendly, able to pass the time of day like normal people. Instead the air between them had been so charged that just one wrong action by her had almost sparked off a war.

Always so sensitive to others she had never experienced such conflicting feelings for anyone before. It was as if she was afraid of him, afraid of his vitality and his commanding presence. For she was far too sensible to be affected by his looks and sheer masculinity.

After about fifteen minutes she ventured back to the poolside, keeping herself shielded from view until her careful glance had made a thorough search of the area. Seeing no sign of Reece Carter she made her way across the warm tiles and to the side of the pool.

Jan was already there, effortlessly performing a length of backstroke with strong, fluid movements of his arms. He caught sight of her, did a half turn under water and swam to the side.

"I thought you weren't coming."

"Sorry," she apologized, once more slipping off her T-shirt. "I got held up. I hoped you'd wait."

"Forever for the fiery English siren." He hauled himself effortlessly from the water and stood before her, his eyes taking a similar route over her to that taken by Reece. Curiously Juliet did not suffer the same prickle of heat.

"I like your swimming cossie. I always think a one-piece is far more seductive than a bikini. It leaves just that bit more for the imagination to feed on. Some of the women here could do well to follow your example instead of squeezing themselves into tiny bikinis."

"I suppose they want to get an all-over tan. I wish I could lie on the beach all day, but with my skin I'd burn to a frazzle."

"I think your tan is very becoming, and I love those freckles across your nose."

"They erupted after I'd sat on the beach for a couple of hours the other day. Alison's so lucky. She can bake all day with no after-effects. Actually the only reason she does it is to weigh up the men. She's looking for a nice man who is not huge, nor flashy."

"And you? Are you looking for a

man? Is that why you asked me to teach you to dive underwater?"

"Of course not. And I didn't ask you. You asked me if you remember. Anyway, I really do want to learn to dive."

"Good. Then let's start."

Jan began with a simple lesson, making her sit on the side of the pool and do breathing exercises.

After that he slipped an oxygen tank onto her back and told her to do the same exercises but with the tube in her mouth. Finally he helped her into the water and took her to the deep end, coaxing her down to the floor of the pool. Just as the first guests began to take up their places on the sunbeds surrounding the pool Juliet managed a very basic underwater dive on her own from the surface of the pool to the blue-tiled floor.

"You learn quickly," Jan complimented as they sat on the side, both dangling their feet in the water. "A couple more lessons here in the pool, and you'll be able to swim underwater for longer spells. The main problems to watch out for then will still be your breathing and economising on energy."

"When will we be able to go in the sea?"

"Patience," he said, holding up his hand. "If you go before you're ready you could risk an accident. When you can swim underwater here in the pool for several minutes, then — and only then — will I consider the sea. If you follow my advice you'll soon be swimming round the coral reefs."

"Have you ever taught any of the other reps?"

"I taught Jane Tyson a thing or two," he said wickedly.

Juliet ignored that. "Do you know Koelle Wiseman?"

"The American heiress who's just filling in time as a rep until she finds herself a rich husband? Yes, I know her. Why?"

"She sailed out with Reece Carter in *Razzmatazz* the other day."

"Mmm, I saw her. She quite often goes out with him."

"They appear to be good friends."

"I should imagine they are. I understand he sold his old boat to her parents last year. Now, he would be a perfect husband for her. Maybe that's why I see her around with him a lot."

"Do you think he wants her around him?"

"Any man in his right mind would want her around him. Now, are you hungry?"

Though the lesson had tired her physically it had also sharpened her appetite. "I'm famished," she told him.

"How about breakfast then? On the terrace? Eggs, bacon? Or we could try the typical Bermudan weekend breakfast of fish with tomato and onion sauce, boiled potatoes and a hard-boiled egg."

It all sounded like manna from heaven to Juliet. She nodded emphatically and they headed for the terraces.

"I would really like to pay you for your time," she told him as they both tucked into the breakfast the waiter laid before them.

"I don't want your money," he replied. "Yes, I'm the teacher and you the pupil, but let's look upon it as a friend teaching another. OK?"

"Jan, that's so good of you."

"Anyway, it makes a change for me to be teaching someone who really wants to learn and who's not after . . . well, shall we say lessons of another nature?"

Juliet was about to raise her fork to her mouth but stopped. "You mean it's true? It really does go on?"

"The rich old widow and the young sports coach, you mean? Of course it does. Mrs Andrina Saville even invited me to her room yesterday."

Juliet stared at him, eyes filling with speculation.

"And I know what you want to ask but daren't. No, of course I didn't. Have you seen her?"

"Yes, the other day," Juliet replied, visions of the platinum blonde wealthy English widow with her jawline hidden by jowls and her small, rotund figure encased in a minuscule bikini that would have given Juliet second thoughts about wearing.

For a moment they stared at each other, then as if on cue they both spluttered into delighted laughter at the thought of Jan getting to grips with Mrs Andrina Saville.

It was at that moment, as she threw back her head in delight, that she saw Reece Carter, on the top floor of the hotel, leaning his arms on the balcony rail. He was looking down at her. The laugh stopped in her throat. How long had he been there, watching her with Jan? She lowered her eyes once more and stared down at her plate covered with the breakfast she had refused to have with him. All of a sudden, she didn't feel hungry any more.

6

JULIET was unusually quiet in the taxi on the way to the Carter's residence. The bank of clouds that she had seen forming on the horizon had now rolled in; dark, grey, forbidding.

"I think it's going to rain," Alison observed glancing at the towering clouds.

"Will it last long?" Juliet enquired.

"No, a short heavy blast of rain, that's all. The sun will be out again by mid-afternoon. How's everything at the Island Cove?"

Juliet picked an imaginary thread from the skirt of her dress. Jenny Carter had told her not to dress up, so she had chosen a plain beige cotton safari outfit which she had dressed up with a wide, brown leather belt and a chunky wooden necklace at her throat.

"Fine. No problems."

"Does that include Reece Carter?"

"No, he's still a problem. Alison, will he be there today?"

"I couldn't say. He doesn't live at the family residence any more. He has an apartment on the top floor of the hotel." She nudged Juliet and leaned across, lowering her voice in confidence. "I know who will be there though."

Juliet returned her smile. "Who?"

"A man I met last week. Paul Stewart. He's a widower and owns one of the most exclusive fashion salons on the island. I went in for a browse and he was so nice I ended up buying myself a dress. I've been in almost every day since." Now her face fell and she sighed. "It's costing me a fortune."

Juliet's mouth dropped open. "Heavens, Alison, you don't mean you're buying something every time you go into his shop?"

"It's not a shop, Juliet," Alison reprimanded. "It's a salon. Paul's one of the elite of Bermuda, along with the Carters. We're fortunate to have been invited for aperitifs."

Confined within an area of about twenty square miles everything on the island of Bermuda is kept on a modest scale so it did not take long to weave along the narrow roads bordered in profusion with bougainvillaea, hibiscus and oleander bushes.

The Carter residence, unlike villas in other countries which are hidden away behind walls and dense foliage, was out in the open, to be viewed by anyone who was passing by. Meticulously groomed lawns surrounded the large, pink-stoned house. White shutters graced the windows and the villa was topped with a white-tiled roof.

It was all set in one of the most attractive surroundings Juliet had ever seen, and she knew that with this kind of ambience and the warm welcome that awaited her from Colin and Jenny Carter she should be looking forward to it. If only someone could tell her whether Reece was going to be there or not, she might be able to settle down.

The antagonism she had felt towards him that morning had largely died down. Whatever he had felt when he had seen her breakfasting with Jan she couldn't begin to imagine, but she suspected his sentiments might lie somewhere in the realms of resentment; and she in turn was suffering dreadfully from guilt.

Shortly after their arrival Jenny ushered Alison and Juliet into the lounge which overlooked the sea. It was richly decorated with a thick carpet square surrounded by highly polished floorboards, and fine pieces of furniture. Everywhere one looked were wonderful little art objects, treasures that Jenny Carter had amassed over the years, from exotic seashells to a miniature replica of a vintage Rolls Royce borrowed from her son.

"I've never seen such a lovely house," Juliet remarked spontaneously to Jenny Carter.

"Why, thank you. We are rather fond of the old place. It's been in the family a long time. Since the beginning of the eighteen hundreds. Now come and meet everyone. You're the last to arrive."

She handed Juliet a glass of wine then drew her towards the rest of the invited guests. A quick study by Juliet revealed no Reece. The anxiety that had weighed her down all that morning was lifted and she began to feel at ease.

"This is my daughter, Sally, and her husband Mason Brent. Juliet Hamilton, the rep for Ultimate Tours at the hotel."

Sally Brent was about two years older than her brother, that is to say around thirty-five years old, but she looked much younger. With her dark hair, blue eyes and strawberries and cream complexion she was vital and alive; qualities that her husband had almost certainly fallen in love with. He stood by her now, maybe a couple of years older than his wife, tall, bespectacled and with a notable twinkle of good humour in his eye.

"Mum always likes to invite the Ultimate Tours girls around occasionally," Sally said. "It's all become sort of a tradition."

"A very thoughtful one," Juliet commented.

"So how long are you here for?" Mason asked. "Have you any idea?"

"None at all. I could be posted elsewhere next month or I might find myself closeted here for the next few years."

"You get to go home in that time, though, don't you?"

"Yes, I was home in March for about a month, and I'm hoping to get home again for Christmas this year."

"And where is home exactly?"

"Do you know England?"

"Just a little," Mason retorted with an amused grin.

"He is English," Sally put in, giving him a reproving dig. "I met him over there whilst I was studying at Bristol Uni."

Juliet returned his smile. "I'm from the north of England, Lancashire actually."

"Snap! So am I. Oh," he sighed, "you don't know how good it is to speak to another human being."

Juliet was startled by such a strange remark, yet she sensed a true feeling of pleasure in Mason's tone. She was thinking of asking him to expand on his curious statement when a car was heard, crunching up the gravel driveway.

"Oh, that will be Paul Stewart," Jenny said moving towards the door.

Juliet glanced across the room at Alison and smiled mischievously. Alison's face turned quite pink.

"Oh!" Jenny's sudden exclamation of surprise sent an inexplicable shiver of foreboding through Juliet. Lowering her glass she watched eagle-eyed as Jenny moved to the entrance of the lounge. "Reece is with him, too," she went on

110

to announce, clearly as surprised by his appearance as Juliet was horrified.

"I didn't think Reece was coming," said Sally to no one in particular.

Juliet's heart began to pound in its cavity. "I didn't expect to see him here, either."

"He doesn't really like these party things Mum and Dad throw on occasions," Sally told her. "He tries to avoid them whenever possible. I wonder what's brought him here today?"

It crossed Juliet's mind to try and summon up some sort of excuse and make her escape, but she had only just arrived and politeness prevented her from taking such an early leave. A nervous perspiration broke out over her body and it occurred to her that she was just as agitated as Alison . . . but for a different reason.

Paul Stewart came in several seconds before Reece. He was not what Juliet had imagined. Of medium height with light brown hair, he was not much more than thirty-five, an unassuming, pleasant-looking man in Bermuda shorts, black jacket and wearing a tie. Juliet noticed he caught sight of Alison and returned her smile quite warmly.

Reece entered the room at the same time as a clap of thunder shook the house. Juliet considered it an appropriate entrance for him.

Dressed casually in cream chino trousers and navy blue short-sleeved shirt he glanced around him quickly, almost searchingly, Juliet thought, then his eyes fell on her. There was a pulse beat of silence, and the penetrating glance he bestowed on her disturbed her in a curious way that heightened all her senses. Then without acknowledging her presence he swung away to return the greetings of the other guests, confirming Juliet's worst fears. He had taken umbrage at having witnessed her enjoying breakfast with Jan after refusing his own invitation.

Outside, the heavens opened and the rain hurtled down furiously, prompting some of the guests to move to the open sliding doors that led onto the terrace and watch as the water swilled down the furrows on the white tiled roof. From there it entered an underground tank to be stored and used when necessary.

Sally took Juliet over to meet Paul Stewart who was chatting with Alison, and Juliet soon realized what it was about him that so fascinated her colleague. Suave and charming, he was the perfect proprietor for a woman's fashion shop. He had a knack of listening to a person as if they were the only one in the room, and when he himself spoke it was with a soft, quiet voice that hinted at shyness of character.

Towards 12.30 most of the guests left. Juliet was thinking of making her own preparations for departure when Alison came over.

"Paul's asked me out to lunch." She shrugged her shoulders. "I don't want to say no. You don't mind making your own way back to the hotel, do you?"

"No, of course not. I'll ring for a taxi. Have a good time."

Alison rolled her eyes in a dramatic display of sheer ecstasy then gripped Juliet's arm and made a low growling noise. "You can be sure of it. See you tomorrow."

Jenny bade the two of them farewell then crossed to where Juliet was picking up her handbag. "So you've been deserted, I see. Will you stay for lunch?"

Juliet opened her mouth to protest, not so much because it was inconvenient. It wasn't. She had nothing planned for the rest of that day except finding a sun lounger and stretching out with a book. Lunch with the Carters would have been a pleasant prospect if Reece had not turned up.

"I won't take no for an answer," Jenny chided. "I know very well you're not on duty today."

In fact she insisted so much that Juliet felt obliged to accept for fear of appearing rude, and allowed Jenny to lead her into the dining-room.

She did not sit next to Reece at lunch. He was between Susan and Sally, and she between Archie and Mason. However he did sit directly opposite her which spoiled the whole meal, for every time she looked up she seemed to find herself glancing in his direction and on more than one occasion his own fierce glance clashed with hers. It was all very uncomfortable.

"Any seconds, Jenny?" Mason asked, running his eyes over the remaining chocolate gateau that sat invitingly a little way down the table from him.

"Of course, dear. Help yourself."

Reece pushed the plate along the table towards him, then slid his glance to Juliet. "What about you, Miss Hamilton? You must still be very hungry." Dryness rustled through his voice.

She looked up quickly, meeting eyes that glinted with mischief, and immediately realized he was out to unsettle her. With difficulty she swallowed the last mouthful of sticky gateau, dabbed the serviette to her mouth and studiously ignored him.

"Have another slice," he suggested smoothly, picking up the knife Mason had just abandoned and holding it poised above the rich chocolate icing.

"No, thank you, I'm . . . "

He cut across her, his eyes and voice encompassing the whole table. "Miss Hamilton told me only this morning that she takes very little breakfast," he announced lightly, then snapped his eyes back to hers, his jaw setting in determination. "Go on," he coaxed, his voice softly persuasive. "Another slice."

No one else heard the truculence in his voice, but it was there, ringing soundly in her own ears. Her cheeks burned in her guilt-ridden face, but she met his gaze squarely, refusing to be intimidated. He was angry, she knew, an anger that was mainly the backlash of what he had witnessed that morning — Jan Peters and herself enjoying breakfast together. Rather than abate during the following hours, his rancour had, if anything, increased and festered inside him. Unsettling her at the table appeared to be his way of getting his own back, appeasing his indignation and soothing his hurt male pride.

"Like all women, Juliet is probably watching her waistline," Jenny said, laughing. "Not that she has any need to." Like everyone else she had clearly not noticed the antagonism in her son's actions for she went on to chat about the perennial problems of weight-watching.

Juliet hardly heard for she was still caught up in Reece's stare like a fly in a spider's web.

"Then how about some fruit," Reece went on relentlessly. "An apple perhaps, or a peach." Lazy with satisfaction at having induced her discomfort he picked up a peach from out of the fruit bowl, tossed it in his hands and presented to her. "The blush on this one is similar to the one on your cheeks."

Juliet's colour heightened even more and confusion came to add its presence to her warring emotions. She couldn't tell whether he was being obliquely complimentary now or downright spiteful.

Unable to tear her gaze away from him she stared at him hard. There was something stubborn and determined in the way Reece was returning her look, and it got her back up just watching him tossing the peach in his hand. However uncomfortable he was making her feel she was not going to succumb to his bullying in order to appease his ruffled male ego. However, though she tried to appear indifferent to his spiteful remarks her hands began trembling so much that she had to clasp them together on her lap beneath the table.

"I don't want anything more," she retorted firmly, and reaching for her glass she dragged her gaze from his and turned to Mason, asking him where in Lancashire he had lived.

Lunch being over Jenny announced that coffee would be served on the terrace. It had stopped raining. The clouds had lifted and the sun reappeared, spearing the sea with its powerful rays. Lawned gardens fell away to the water's edge where a small sea-going yacht was moored.

"Is that your yacht, Mr Carter?" she asked Colin.

"Yes, that's *Looking Good*. Not quite in the same league as *Razzmatazz*, eh? But more my style."

"Have you sailed far in her?"

"Just around the islands. It's enough for me."

From here Archie joined the conversation and the talk moved to matters more technical and nautical. Mason turned to Juliet.

"How are you liking it here?"

"It's paradise, isn't it?"

"Do you really think so?" He eyed her carefully. "You're a Lancashire lass.

I thought northern folk were supposed to speak plainly."

Juliet frowned, not understanding his remark. "What do you mean? Don't you think of it as paradise?"

Mason considered her question for a moment. "I think for the tourists it is paradise, and for the people who live here also . . . " There was another pensive silence. "I'm not explaining myself very well. If you're an outsider, like me, it's not the paradise everyone makes it out to be."

Juliet stared up at him questioningly and he went on. "It's oozing with British reserve over here, and trying to cut your way in to the high society that makes up the population is like trying to cut through rock."

"But you're married to Sally. She's Bermudan."

"And it's because of her and who she is that I've been accepted. I would never have done it on my own. Don't get me wrong, Juliet. They're friendly people out here, but if you weren't born here . . . it's a closed society."

"It's always difficult in any society for an outsider to be accepted. But I can imagine what you mean. How did you get on with Reece when you first came here?" she asked, wanting to compare Mason's initial evaluation of his brother-in-law with her own.

"Reece? Oh, no problems at all. The whole family has been marvellous — well, you can see for yourself what kind of people Jenny and Colin are — and Reece is my best friend."

Now a frown passed across Juliet's face. It appeared that Reece Carter got on well with just about everyone he met. So what was it about her that made him so aggressive? There were certainly things about him she didn't like and yet when he looked at her sometimes — and especially this morning by the pool and just now across the table — there was just something in his glances that sent a strange heat creeping over her.

"Have you and Sally any children?"

"No. Not by choice, either." He shrugged, and although his face remained pleasantly impassive Juliet could sense an underlying desperation in him. "It's just that nothing's happened."

"I am sorry. That must be awful for you . . . " Juliet paused, feeling uncomfortable on this topic. She didn't want to brush it off lightly, but neither did she want to appear insensitive or uninterested. "Maybe one day . . . do you live near here?"

"Everyone lives near to each other in Bermuda," he laughed. "Just the other side of the island. I've got a boat firm. I started it up back in England then transferred it over here when Sal and I married. Reece bought his first boat from me. Now he's gone on to bigger and better things."

"Yes, I saw *Razzmatazz* the other day. She's quite super, isn't she?"

"Why don't you get him to take you out in her?" he suggested, clearly believing there was nothing more simple than asking his amiable brother-in-law for a trip around the bay. "I'm sure he'd be delighted."

Juliet's toes curled in her shoes, but she returned his smile. "I'm sure he would," she agreed with veiled sarcasm.

A short while later Juliet announced that she really must return to the hotel. Archie and Susan suggested they all share a taxi back, but Jenny pressed the Fairweathers to spend the rest of the day with them which they readily agreed to do.

"And what about you, dear?" Susan said to Juliet. "You're welcome to stay, too."

"That's so kind of you," Juliet replied. "But I really must be getting back."

"All right, if you're sure. Would you like me to phone for a taxi?"

"That won't be necessary," intervened Reece before Juliet could answer. "I'm going back to the hotel. I'll drop her off."

7

THE afternoon was hot and sticky as a result of the heavy downpour, but the sun shone onto the wet foliage giving rise to a pungent smell of grass and earth.

Along the narrow lanes Reece drove his white, low-slung, open-topped Morgan at a speed in excess of the mandatory twenty miles per hour. Juliet couldn't see the point of owning such a sporty little car that could never be given the chance to show off its performance. Like *Razzmatazz* she decided it was just another show of exhibitionism.

"Of course, going directly back to the hotel won't give you much chance to see the island," Reece was saying.

"I have seen quite a bit of it on my travels," she told him.

"Yes, but only the route from the hotel to the airport. Which is a tiny corner of Bermuda."

Without warning he branched off onto a side road. As the island was no more than a mile across at its widest point it was almost possible to see the sea at all times.

He told her a bit about the history of Bermuda and about the 150 islands that form its archipelago. Apparently the population of about 57,000 people was made up of whites and blacks, the predominant being black.

"It's actually one of the world's richest countries if you look at it in perspective, and with the mild climate and pink beaches is it any wonder we call it Seventh Heaven? But having said that, we don't have everything." His mouth relaxed, permitting a fleeting smile that brought a certain warmth to his lean face. "We don't have skyscrapers, parking meters, pollution, slums. Neither do we have income tax! Do you mind if we make a slight detour? There's somewhere I have to go."

"No, Mr Carter, that's fine," she replied. Not that she could say anything else. She had no idea where they were and should she have asked him to set her down now, she would have been completely lost.

He let his gaze stray from the winding lane to rest on her, briefly skimming over her. "We're not at the hotel now. Why don't we call each other by our first names when we're both off duty?"

"As you wish," she replied with indifferent compliance. She really couldn't see herself ever addressing this overbearing man by his first name.

With her elbow resting on the window frame and her fist pressed to her mouth, Juliet stared at the passing scenery as if she had seen it all before. Her thoughts were in chaos. He was being unbelievably pleasant all of a sudden, as if the moment of festering rancour he had displayed over lunch had never happened.

They continued along winding lanes

free of litter, graffiti and any signs of vandalism. Long, sandy beaches in shades of white and pink occasionally came into view, and the brochure-blue sea could always be found on either one side or the other.

In due course the road ran out at a pair of wrought iron gates. Reece climbed out of the low-slung car and unlocked them. Then they were moving slowly along a driveway lined with palm and banana saplings and speckled with the ubiquitous hibiscus and oleander bushes. The drive curved to the right then suddenly opened out to reveal a large one-storey villa.

Obviously newly-built with small mounds of rubble still waiting to be cleared away, it seemed to be the end of the line for the time being and when Reece climbed out, Juliet automatically followed, her glance taking in the impressive bungalow.

"Come on and we'll have a look around," said Reece, leading the way to the front door. He fished in his trouser pockets, withdrew a key and inserted it in the lock. The door opened into a hallway and Juliet stepped onto the polished wood floor. As she had expected the house was completely empty — no rugs, no furniture, no curtains, not even any fittings — and the all-pervading smell of newness hung in the air.

For the next few minutes she dutifully followed him round in silence, her indifferent gaze automatically skimming over the dimensions of the rooms, noting their shape, and the position of the windows.

"Would you make any changes?" he asked her suddenly, emerging from the room that was destined to be the kitchen. He stood in the doorway, filling it with his tall frame.

Juliet was off guard, unprepared for such a question. She stared at him, taking in the vitality that stamped his features.

"Mr Carter, it's not — "

"Reece, please," he insisted.

Her teeth nibbled nervously at her bottom lip. She took a breath and said carefully, "Reece, it's not for me to say." His name was new and strange on her lips.

"But if it was yours." He put the statement to her as he moved round the dining-room, tossing the house keys nonchalantly in his hand whilst checking over the light fittings, switches and plugs. "What would you do with it?"

"Well . . . " her gaze made a sweeping assessment of the room, "not a lot in here. But the kitchen . . . well, there I'd have it fitted with old pine units, a large sink and built-in appliances with spotlights shining on tiled work surfaces. And the bathroom . . . I think I'd have light-coloured fitments installed in there. Perhaps something in champagne or oyster. And the en suite bathroom, possibly the palest blue to give an impression of coolness seeing as the main bedroom faces south . . . and in the bedroom I'd have coordinated linen and curtains in blue and white, and a big kingsize bed on the main wall . . . " She stopped suddenly. She was getting carried away, and there was something intense about the way he was looking at her. "Of course, that's only my opinion," she concluded with a shrug.

He nodded in implied acceptance, stepped to the sliding doors of the dining-room and invited her to view the terrace. A tear-shaped swimming pool, tiled in blue, rippled gently in the soft, warm breeze, and just below the terrace a deserted beach dazzled white in the sun.

"So what is your overall impression?" asked Reece, coming over to stand by the terrace rail.

"It's all very nice," she retorted, refusing to be drawn again. They were like a young couple in the throes of house hunting. "Is it yours?"

"Not yet. I'm thinking of buying it."

Juliet's glance was sharp in its

assessment of him. "When a man thinks about buying a house like this he must be considering settling down and starting a family."

"It's up to me to give my parents the pleasure of having grandchildren."

"Yes, Mason told me he and Sally had no children."

Reece turned round and leaned both arms on the rail. His gaze took in the wide expanse of ocean and the coral reefs over which the water rose and fell gently. "It's not by design. They've been married for twelve years without results."

"There's time yet."

Reece twisted his mouth doubtfully. "Sally is two years older than I am. At thirty-five she hasn't an awful lot of time left."

"They're very happy together, though, I can tell."

"Yes, I envy them their life together." A long silence followed, then he let his gaze stray from the ocean to briefly rest on her, skimming over her. "And what about you, Juliet? Are you manhunting too, like Alison?"

"Indeed I'm not! Alison's idea of a husband is one who's youngish, good-looking and rich. I'm not in the market for rich men. I'm the kind of person who still has romantic daydreams and I prefer to stick with them at the moment."

"All culled from reading books, no doubt."

"Reading is what I do in my spare time, although I have been spending quite some time in the sun."

"Have you done any scuba-diving yet?"

"No. I am learning though."

"Oh?" In her side vision Juliet saw him turn round, lean an arm on the rail and study her profile. "You're taking lessons?"

"Yes, Jan Peters is an excellent teacher."

"In more ways than one," Reece muttered quietly.

The muted sarcasm in his voice

made Juliet turn away from the sea. She met his gaze questioningly, but it was cool and veiled, not sustaining the remark he had just made.

"I'm only taking up scuba-diving. I don't know very much about him. But I believe he's prolific in most sporting activities."

It was an artless remark that prompted a wry smile which emphasized the sensual line of his mouth. He didn't attempt to hide the speculation in his gaze. "Jan must find you an avid pupil if he's neglecting the other guests."

There was a hidden meaning there that Juliet wasn't too sure she wanted to understand. "Jan is teaching me in his spare time. That is why I was at the pool so early this morning."

"And what form does the payment take?"

The taunting comment went through her like an electric shock and she suddenly lost patience with this cross-talk. She had answered him in a straightforward manner and all he was doing was playing on her words with suggestive innuendos.

"There is no payment, Mr Carter." She addressed him formally to show her displeasure and to push her point home. "No payment whatsoever."

His immobility was broken by a surge of rippling energy as he pushed himself up from the terrace rail. The sudden movement suggested a slight irritation with himself for asking such a leading question, and the gruffness of his voice backed up this impression. He glanced at his watch. "I'll take you back to the hotel."

Leaving the villa they set off back towards the hotel on the northernmost point of the island. As they continued along the road Juliet noticed that there seemed to be no social order in the houses they now passed.

On the whole the villas on the right, nearest the beach and with spectacular views across the bays, were large, meticulously tended, and obviously very expensive. On the left were smaller, shabbier cottages, nestling on the hillsides, with untended gardens filled with black children. The air, no longer scented with the sweet smell of earth and flowers, now held the more pungent aroma of spices.

They followed the causeway across the harbour to St George's Island. Though the sky was clear, the wind had started to get up again. Reece pointed out the reefs. What only a short time before had been a calm swell was now a churning, boiling foam. Even towards the shore, the wind-whipped water held enough force to make surf on the beaches.

Signs began to appear indicating the close proximity of the Island Cove Hotel. Reece drove up to the main entrance and slotted the showy Morgan into a parking lot.

"Thank you for the lift back," said Juliet. "And for the tour of the island. I think the villa's beautiful, and I think you should go ahead and buy it."

Her statement was meant to ease

any remaining tension between them, and her offering was accepted. A smile gentled the angles of his features.

"Then I'll phone the agent first thing tomorrow morning." Juliet experienced a tingling of alarm. Was he really going to splash out goodness knows how many hundreds of thousands of dollars on a house, just on her say-so?

"Don't just go on my advice."

"Why not? It so happens that I agreed with everything you had to say about it."

She leaned back in the bucket-shaped seat of the luxurious sports car. "I hope your future wife will like it, whoever she may be."

"Oh, I'm sure she will."

They both climbed out of the car and Juliet began to make her way towards the gardens and her cool, pretty, welcoming bungalow.

"Juliet," Reece called and she stopped, half turning to face him. He stood with one foot on the lower stoop of the steps leading to the darkened plate glass doors. "When do you next have a diving lesson?"

"Tomorrow morning."

He nodded, staring at her in pensive thought. "Don't lose your head, will you?"

Juliet watched him run up the steps and disappear into the foyer of the hotel. She was unsure of this change in him from arrogant proprietor to cynical observer to elder brother. She liked none of these attitudes. What she wanted from him was something in between, like the times he chatted to her about the fish in the sea, the island, and what he could do with the villa. In fact, before he had got onto the subject of Jan she had felt very at ease standing on the terrace with him, gazing at the beach below and the crystal sea.

A rather capricious thought now crossed her mind, and she found herself wondering what her reaction might have been if he had suddenly turned to her, slid his arms about her and kissed her. A frisson ran down her back at the thought, and she knew she couldn't even understand her own attitude, never mind his.

That evening Juliet was tucked away in the corner of the L-shaped reception desk. Remembering what Koelle had told her about the time she had discovered two names were missing off her list of incoming guests Juliet had decided to compare the hotel's list for the following week with her own to ensure that there were no omissions.

There were several guests at the reception desk and many more were walking through the area en route to the restaurants. She was vaguely aware that someone had come to stand at the corner of the desk but it was several seconds before she felt the touch of their gaze and realized she was being watched.

She turned suddenly, seeing Reece leaning an elbow on the desk, surprising him and catching the intensity in his look before he wiped it away. Instead of the casual clothes he had worn earlier that day he was now dressed in a cream-jacketed dinner suit and black tie. There was a swift, hot rise of her pulse.

"I didn't think you were on duty today," he remarked.

"I'm not," she replied, caught up in the masculine aura he was presenting. "I just thought I'd check over next week's guests. When I was at the airport the other day I suddenly had a dreadful thought. What if the names on my list didn't match those of the incoming passengers?"

Reece smiled, the corners of his mouth deepening. "It very rarely happens. And if ever it does, don't panic. We'll sort out something." He paused now, his eyes skimming her face. "Have you anything arranged for the rest of the evening?"

"No." Juliet shook her head. "I thought I'd have an early night."

"Ah." He nodded sagely. "Very sensible." In the short silence that followed he seemed on the verge of saying something else, but the receptionist came over to him. He looked away from Juliet, giving the young woman his attention.

"I'm off to the Yacht Club, Joanne. I'll be away all evening and I may be late in coming back. Mr Scarlet will deal with any queries."

"Very good, Mr Carter. Have a pleasant evening."

He turned back to Juliet, paused a moment as if considering a sudden idea, then changed his mind.

"I'll say goodnight, then," he said, and accompanied it with a smile so unforced, so unexpected that it stunned Juliet into silence. Digging the car keys from out of his pocket he walked from the foyer out into the evening sunshine.

As the automatic doors closed behind him, Juliet released the breath she had been unconsciously holding. She couldn't get that smile out of her mind. In fact it affected her so much that she was unable to concentrate on her task. All fingers and thumbs she fumbled clumsily through the sheets of paper as she bent her head to the lists once more. Somewhere in the hazy distance she heard the chatter of the two receptionists.

"What's going on at the Yacht Club, then?"

"It's the annual members' dinner, I think. The Governor will be there and all the top people."

"Who's Mr Carter going with?"

"I'll give you one guess."

The other young woman giggled. "Oooh, now let me see. It couldn't, by any chance, be K.W.?"

"How did you guess?" Again they giggled, delighted to find themselves on the same wavelength. "That's why he'll be back late. Very late, by my guess. Like tomorrow morning."

The initials K.W. were not lost on Juliet, and the mention of them hit a raw nerve. She stood absolutely still. She knew all too well what the receptionists were hinting at. She had suspected it for a few days and now she knew. Reece and Koelle Wiseman were much more than friends; and she was suddenly tormented by images of Reece in the arms of the stunning, blonde American girl.

The intensity of her feelings shocked her. If she had been confused about her own attitude she wasn't any longer. It was crazy, but it was true. She was jealous.

The next morning, at seven o'clock, Jan took her down to the deserted beach, slipped an oxygen tank onto her back and meticulously taught her how to breathe through the mouthpiece. Then he led her into the sea and coaxed her to swim out of her depth, under the water. A short while later she was diving to a depth of ten feet, controlling her breathing and moving gracefully through the water. Even at this shallow depth there was plenty to see — small fish that darted around the rocks, florets of coral — and when she finally surfaced she felt exhilarated.

"We must have been under hours," she said, once more on the beach and slipping off the oxygen tank.

"Just half an hour, that's all. It's enough for your first dive. Any problems?"

"None at all. Jan, it was fabulous down there. I don't think I've done anything so exciting in my life."

"You can see why I spend most of my spare time diving."

"Yes, I can't wait to go out to the reefs."

He put up his hand, indicating for her to control her impatience. "The time will come. Another lesson in the shallower water, then we'll take a boat out and I'll show you how to dive in."

"Backwards," she told him.

He raised his eyebrows in a wry gesture. "So who's been watching the films on T.V. then?"

She laughed with him and sat down on the sand, allowing the warm sun to dry her skin.

143

"Jan, do you work here independently?"

"No, I'm paid by the hotel."

"So the guests don't actually give you payment?"

"Not by the lesson, no. Most of them tip me generously before they leave. It pads out my wage and enables me to buy first class diving gear." He leaned over her, brushing a strand of hair from out of her face. "Why?"

"Just a thought that crossed my mind. And are most of your pupils women?"

"Without exception. They like the idea of having the sole attention of a young, bronzed man for an hour."

"What age range in general do you teach?"

"Some are married women whose husbands have forgotten how to flatter them; others are widows who have no man to pay them attention. If they want to learn to play tennis, then I teach them tennis. If they want to learn to swim, I teach them to swim. And if they want me to pay them compliments, then I do that too. Their wish is my command. For the healthy tip I'll get at the end of their stay, I'll do anything." He shot her a sideways glance. "Does that shock you?"

Juliet sat in pensive thought, drawing circles in the sand with her finger and matching what Jan had just told her to Reece's half-veiled comments. Jan was clearly a man without reservations. But she still found his company pleasant. He was also a good teacher, taking her step by step through the basic art of underwater diving. She reckoned she could overlook his lack of scruples.

"You're a nice person, Jan. We get on well together. That's how I want it to stay."

The grin he gave her made him look almost boyish. He began to gather their diving gear together.

"Do you think Reece Carter will marry Koelle Wiseman?" Juliet queried, folding up the towels.

"It's on the cards, I should imagine. Can you take the masks while I carry the tanks?" he asked.

"Of course." She took them from him and shook off the excess sea water.

"Thanks. I'll rinse them out under the fresh water tap when we get to the gardens."

Juliet glanced around to make sure they hadn't left anything. "She doesn't seem right for him, though."

"No, I agree. She's attractive and showy, but shallow." He picked up the heavy oxygen tanks and started back up the beach. "But who are we to pass judgement on his choice? Come on and we'll grab a bite to eat before I have to meet my first pupil."

8

IT was just after 8.30 the same morning when Juliet hurried into the foyer of the hotel. It was promising to be a long day because along with her own duties she had also agreed to take on Alison's later that day at the Coral Reef Hotel.

Paul Stewart's elegant salon beneath the shady arcades that lined the Hamilton harbour front was giving a fashion show of its latest chic imports that afternoon, to the wives of Bermuda's well-heeled businessmen. The governor's wife was expected to be present, so Alison had asked Juliet to swap duties so that she could accept Paul's invitation to attend.

Juliet's first duty that day was to escort guests, whose holiday had ended, to the airport. She found a comfortable chair in a corner and sat down to wait for them to congregate. She didn't want to give the impression she had nothing to do so she looked through the day's schedule, glancing from time to time at her watch.

It wasn't long before the lifts brought the first guests. They spilled out in a jumbled confusion of suitcases, bags, mementos of their stay, and fretful children who got under the feet of their even more irritable parents.

Juliet stood up and went to meet them, smiling warmly and sympathizing with them that their holiday had all too soon come to an end.

As she led them across the foyer and pointed out where they could leave their things whilst they went in for breakfast, the automatic doors slid open, bringing warm air scented with mimosa to mingle with the air-conditioned coolness.

Juliet glanced up. Reece Carter stood in the entrance, his tall, athletic frame silhouetted against the bright light of the morning sun. Juliet's carefully ordered thoughts suddenly went haywire, not least of all because Reece was still wearing the same clothes as he had worn the previous night.

To Juliet's over-imaginative mind there was only one explanation for this. That he had spent the night somewhere with Koelle — perhaps in that glorious sea-facing bedroom at the beautiful villa Juliet had looked around only the previous day where she had offered him her ideas on decor and fitments.

Of course there was no bed, no furniture, nothing in the house, not even plumbing; but what was that minor inconvenience to a couple who couldn't wait to get their hands on each other?

Someone asked her what time the minibus was due to leave and she answered them automatically, without a thought to their question. What did it matter if Reece had spent the night with Koelle? And why was she bothering about it anyway?

Fraternization between employees was frowned upon but Reece and Koelle were friends — more than friends — and Reece wrote the rules anyway, so it was perfectly acceptable for him to break them.

Reece's all-encompassing glance skimmed the huge foyer, found the small group of bronzed tourists and settled on Juliet. He moved across to her. Juliet fought to push the images of Reece and Koelle in each other's arms from her mind.

"Good morning, Miss Hamilton." He addressed her formally, even briskly, which did not help her overwrought state. It was as if all the warmth he had displayed towards her yesterday had been lost and forgotten in Koelle's arms.

"Good morning." She forced a tight little smile to her lips and searched his dark face — looking for what, she did not know. How was a person supposed to look after making love all night? The shadow around his chin indicated he had not shaved and she imagined he looked rather tired, just as one would with very little sleep.

She wondered how often they spent the night together. She pictured them again, together. She seemed to delight in torturing herself. She couldn't bear such imaginings, and yet she couldn't stop herself from creating them.

She looked away, avoiding his unrelenting stare for fear his shrewd eyes might read the turmoil in her.

"I thought Miss Gregory was on airport duty today," he commented.

There was a dreadful confusion in her head that she couldn't search through. Her thoughts were whirling too fast.

"Mr Stewart took her to the Yacht Club dinner, last night, and she only got back an hour ago. She's going to one of his fashion shows this afternoon, so I agreed to swap rotas so that she could get some sleep," she explained, trying to keep her voice from trembling, and failing dismally.

Reece nodded his head whilst running

a curious glance over her flushed face, then transferred his attention to the guests. His face broke into a warm, friendly smile and he suddenly became the urbane and charming hotel proprietor, enquiring as to whether they had enjoyed their stay and wishing them a safe journey back to London.

Juliet could hardly believe the change from cool, distant employer to considerate host. She wondered what his reaction to herself might have been had she been on the other side of the fence — a guest paying two thousand pounds a week into his coffers.

Reece swung round, focusing his intent grey gaze on Juliet once more. "Have they had breakfast, Miss Hamilton?"

"No, not yet."

"Then you'd better get them to the restaurant if the bus arrives at 9.30."

It was possibly meant as a statement more than a command, but Juliet saw it as yet another display of no-confidence in her abilities to organize. She wanted to tell him that the guests would have been enjoying their breakfast right now if he hadn't intercepted them, but fought down the impulse. Such a retort would create yet more tension which would be sensed by the guests, and above all they must leave the hotel with a good impression.

"What time is their plane?" Reece asked.

"Midday."

"And after the airport?" He peered at her questioningly. "Where are you then?"

"At the Coral Reef for the rest of the day."

"I see." Reece let an interval of silence lapse. "And what time do you finish there?"

She paused now, realizing his line of questioning was taking a different, more personal course. She glanced at the group of guests chatting amongst themselves whilst they waited patiently for her to complete her conversation with the hotel's proprietor, then looked up at him, meeting the level glance of his grey eyes.

"Well," she faltered, "I'm due to have lunch there. Then there's some paperwork to do. I have to phone Ultimate Tours in London . . . and do Alison's enquiries . . . " Her clipboard slipped from beneath her arm and she went to catch it. It gave her a convenient distraction, and an excuse to avoid Reece's eyes. "So I should think it will be getting on for about five o'clock."

"And then you'll be coming back here?" It was a prompting question.

"Yes . . . I should think so . . . "

"Good."

That made her lift her gaze again and she suddenly saw all the things she had been trying so hard not to notice. He was handsome, lean, suntanned, vigorous. In his white dinner jacket and black tie, his dark hair stylishly groomed, he was the final product of manhood, suave, charming and immaculately dressed.

"Did you know there's a spectacular floor show here tonight? At nine o'clock?"

"I had heard, yes."

"Steel bands, calypso dancers, limbo dancers," he told her.

Juliet's heart began to pound in its cavity. What was he getting at? Was he asking her to go with him? She hardly dared consider it.

"I don't know . . . I'll see how things go . . ."

Reece swept aside her non-committal remark. "I'd be pleased if you'd be there, Miss Hamilton. It is expected."

Expected! What was this? A court summons? Juliet's moment of elation was crushed by an overwhelming disappointment, and for a stunned second she looked up at him speechlessly. His voice was a sharp reminder that it was an order, and that he expected orders — even those veiled by pleasantries — to be obeyed.

Rebellion licked through her, sparked by his authoritative command, and she would have refused out of sheer stubbornness but for the fact that the evening's entertainment promised to be fun and she had already decided to go before he had mentioned it. Without giving him the satisfaction of a definite answer she turned to the milling group of guests and herded them into the restaurant for their last meal in Seventh Heaven.

The rest of the day was so hectic that she had no time to dwell on Reece Carter's arrogant attitude. But her thoughts did occasionally turn to Koelle Wiseman. In fact, during a snatched lunch she could hardly get her out of her troubled mind. Just how strong were Reece's feelings towards the American girl? Certainly Koelle was in a better position to keep him interested, having enticed him into her bed. Juliet finally arrived back at her bungalow exhausted, troubled and fit for nothing.

Wearily she took off her clothes and showered, allowing a stream of lukewarm water to soothe her hot, tired body. Then wrapping her hair in a towel and slipping into a towelling robe she opened the sliding doors and sat in the privacy of the tiny patio, feet up on the wall and relishing a refreshing cup of tea.

Alison came over about seven o'clock bubbling about the afternoon she had spent at Paul's elegant salon and enthusing over the top people who had attended. Then she brought out a small box and opened it to display a hand-crafted coral necklace.

"Paul gave it to me," she announced.

"It's beautiful." Juliet took it from her and studied it carefully.

"In Bermuda, coral is protected by law, but somehow Paul managed to have this made for me."

"He must think a lot of you then," Juliet commented, handing it back.

"Oh, I hope so. I think he's terrific. I'm just a bit wary, though, of taking everything too fast and frightening him off."

"I don't think you've anything to fear on that score," remarked Juliet. "If he's given you such a beautiful necklace I think he's way past the dithering stage."

Alison sat forward in her chair, eyes alight with eager anticipation. "Honestly? Do you think so?"

Juliet laughed, marvelling how much an outsider could read into a relationship when those concerned seemed so blind. Alison leaned back once more in her chair, closed her eyes and tilted her face up to the evening sky, engrossed in her intense happiness. Juliet went to make another cup of tea in the small kitchenette.

"How was your day?" Alison queried as Juliet set down two mugs on the table between them.

"Busy."

"Thanks for covering for me. You know I'll do it for you sometime." Alison straightened up in her chair, took the mug and sipped at the hot tea. "By the way, I saw Reece Carter on the way over here this evening. He told me to remind you about the floorshow at nine o'clock tonight. Are you going?"

A shock wave went through Juliet. Whether it was because she had for the time being forgotten about the show, or whether it was because Reece was stubbornly ensuring she would obey his command, she didn't know. But his reminder brought a sudden tremble to her hands and she put down her mug of tea in case she spilled any.

"I don't know," she replied in answer to Alison's question. "I haven't decided. Are we expected to go? Is it compulsory?"

"Well, I'm going. But that's because Paul asked me to. And it will be a good show. The Island Cove Hotel is noted for its spectacular entertainment." Alison paused, running a probing gaze over Juliet's agitated face. "What's the matter? Don't you want to go?"

Juliet didn't reply. Her heart was thudding so much that she could hear the blood pounding through her ears.

"How are things going between you and Reece?" Alison queried tactfully.

"All very tricky," Juliet answered.

"Oh? Why?"

With a sudden surge of energy Juliet stood up, wrapped her arms about herself and rubbed them with her hands as if to ward off a chill in the air.

"I think I'm in love with him," she announced flatly.

"My God!" Alison sat bolt upright, her eyes almost popping out of her head. "You're kidding!"

Juliet shook her head and walked to the end of the small patio where she pressed her forehead against the cool stone wall. Reece Carter was searing her very edges and reaching into the nether regions of her soul. He was a man like no other she had known, more powerful, more independent and more alluring.

"I heard you'd been seen with him," Alison commented.

"Oh?" Juliet straightened up, swinging a narrowed gaze round on her colleague.

"And where did you hear that?"

"I don't know now." Alison shrugged. The source didn't seem important. "Just general gossip I suppose from the hotel staff. When you live in such a tightly knit community like a hotel it's impossible to keep anything quiet. And you know how employees like to gossip and speculate about their employers." She peered hard at Juliet. "Is it true? Have you been seeing him?"

"I haven't seen him any more than anyone else," Juliet told her.

"Well, sometimes it doesn't even need a meeting to fall in love," Alison explained. She ran a concerned eye over her friend, seeing the agitation, the restlessness, hearing the nervous tremor in her voice, and realizing it was not exactly the happiest moment of Juliet's life. "Well, I think it's marvellous," she said briskly, her tone full of rebuke. "You're in love, Juliet. In love with the most eligible bachelor in Bermuda. He's young, good-looking and wealthy — what else could you ask for? I think it's wonderful."

"No, it's not," Juliet countered. "He's arrogant, insensitive, conceited . . . "

Alison allowed a moment's silence to pass. "Oh, lordy! You really are in love with him, aren't you? And it's not reciprocated?"

"Of course it's not!" Juliet flung her hands out in despair. "He's hanging around with Koelle Wiseman and from what I've heard it's all pretty serious."

"Well . . . " Alison demurred, "I must admit that I'd heard that, too. Wedding bells have been mentioned in passing . . . " She shrugged, giving a lame little laugh. "The same source, mind you. The staff."

Juliet began pacing again, Alison's words having reinforced her realization that Koelle Wiseman was a bigger obstacle than she had first thought.

"He spent last night with her," Juliet announced grimly.

Alison looked suddenly startled, then blinked. "He certainly did not," she retorted and Juliet stopped her pacing,

162

eyes fixed intently on Alison.

"He went to the Royal Bermuda Yacht Club," Juliet informed her, "and didn't come home until after eight this morning."

"That's right." Alison nodded her head vigorously. "But he arrived alone, yesterday evening, and left alone this morning shortly after breakfasting at the club. I know, Juliet, because I was there. Remember? With Paul. It was the annual dinner and it usually goes on all night, spilling over into breakfast for the more hardy ones. Reece spent some of the time with Paul and me, and believe me, he had no escort. He was entirely alone. Actually, I kept wondering why he had no partner. Sometimes I thought he looked a bit lost."

Juliet flushed at her embarrassing surmise. She suddenly recalled him asking her whether she had anything arranged for that evening, and then the way he had paused as if wanting to say something further. Had he been considering asking her to accompany him? No, it wasn't possible, she decided. Member or not, one just did not turn up on the spur of the moment at one of these elite affairs with an extra guest in tow.

"Well, anyway," she went on resolutely, "he's still thinking of buying a beautiful villa over on Main Island. I saw it the other day. He took me there, showed me around and asked what I thought of it. Why did he do that, Alison? Why did he ask me for advice about a house he was buying for himself and Koelle?"

Hearing the hurt in Juliet's voice Alison rolled to her feet and slipped an arm around Juliet's shoulder, giving her a comforting hug. "Don't you think your imagination's working overtime?"

"But everyone knows about Koelle and Reece. And you said yourself that you'd heard wedding bells ringing," Juliet protested.

"But it is all gossip, after all's said and done. Listen, if you've got it so badly, why don't you sound him out?"

Juliet's eyes narrowed. "What do you mean?"

"Give him a hint about the way you feel."

Juliet's mouth fell open in horror. "And have him stare down at me in that superior way of his whilst telling me brusquely that a relationship is out of the question?" Juliet shook her head, causing the chestnut waves to fall about her face. "I couldn't do that. I just couldn't. I'd die!"

"It might be worth a try," Alison coaxed. "Men just cannot resist the idea of a woman being in love with them. It inflates their egos."

For a moment Juliet stared unseeing at Alison as images of standing before Reece and declaring her love for him danced grotesquely before her eyes. The very idea horrified her and again she shook her head.

"He'd ask for my transfer and I couldn't bear that. The humiliation, the rejection, not seeing him again . . . "

"Then you have to ask yourself a question," Alison told her. "Would it be better if you told him how you feel and risk being transferred, or stay silent and watch his relationship with Koelle blossom maybe into marriage? Who knows," she concluded archly, "you might even get an invitation to the wedding."

Juliet turned away in miserable silence, toying with a small stone with the toe of her sandal. "I don't want to leave here," she said eventually in a quiet voice that trembled with emotion.

"Then you're just going to have to suffer in silence," Alison reasoned with little sympathy. "You have only yourself to blame."

And suddenly Juliet knew she had to see him that evening, even if it was just a glimpse. The way she was feeling, it was as if he had got under her skin and now she couldn't get him out. All she could think about was him, Reece, and what it might feel like to be held in his arms . . .

Apart from the beige safari dress she had worn to the Carter's house for lunch, and her two uniform outfits, Juliet had one other dress, a more formal one in a pale blue fine cotton lawn with thin shoulder straps and a wide border of broderie anglaise around the bodice and hem. It had a full skirt which she wore several inches above the knee to show off her good legs.

She arrived on the large terrace to the hotel just before nine o'clock to the accompaniment of the inch-long tree frogs that chirped like bells. The palms and banana trees were strung with coloured lights and all the tables carried candles surrounded by floral decorations. Waiters weaved expertly around the tables carrying trays of refreshments from the bar to the terrace.

Someone waving frantically from a table situated close to the entertainment area caught Juliet's eye and in the dimness she could make out Susan Fairweather beckoning her over. As she wended her way through the maze of tables she saw that it was a large gathering which she had been invited to join with several tables pushed together to make one big one. In one glance she spotted the Carters, Sally and Mason, the Fairweathers, Paul and Alison — but no Reece.

The stab of disappointment she felt by his absence was tempered by the fact that there was still a spare chair opposite her own, and a few moments later a tall figure dressed in white slacks and a brightly patterned shirt of Bermuda-made cloth emerged from the hotel onto the terrace and moved towards the group.

Juliet watched Reece approach, tall, lean, vital, so masculine. He acknowledged everyone with cheerful greetings, kissed his mother on the cheek then sat down opposite Juliet. As he greeted her she saw his gaze run swiftly over her, taking in the blue eyes enhanced by the lightly tanned skin, and the attractive flush to her cheeks which complemented her dark chestnut hair.

Juliet returned the stare, gazed into the dark intensity of his eyes and ached inside. She slowly became aware of a certain stillness around them, as if the others were watching the exchange. Then someone spoke, immediately claiming Reece's attention.

"Is Koelle not coming tonight?" asked Mason.

"She's working until eleven o'clock. She'll be over later," Reece informed the group.

Juliet looked away, finding a timely distraction in the roll of drums that announced the start of the evening's floorshow. The entertainment began with fiery, acrobatic limbo dancers whose black, gleaming bodies writhed and bent into the most incredible positions. After that a steel band took over. Mason and Sally stood up to dance the rumba, and Susan

Fairweather asked Reece if he'd like to have a go. A moment later Juliet was surprised to feel a tap on her shoulder and turning round she found Jan standing behind her. He asked her to dance.

"Not the rumba, mind you," he warned, flicking a glance at the couples on the terrace who were expertly displaying their skills. "I'm not into Latin American stuff. But maybe we can make up some steps as we go along."

He smiled cheerfully, but for the first time ever Juliet felt irritated by Jan's presence and fought to hide her feelings from him. She stood up and allowed him to lead her onto the floor.

"You look gorgeous tonight," he complimented.

"Thank you. I wasn't sure what to wear. Everyone seems to dress quite formally. When I was in Spain everyone wore shorts, even to dinner at night. Here in Bermuda dressing for dinner is almost standard."

"Decorum is more pronounced here than in other countries, especially in a high-class hotel like this. Chalk it up to British reserve." He glanced back over his shoulder to the Carter gathering. "How come you're sitting with the elite of Bermuda?"

"I was invited to."

"Lucky you! Getting in with the Carters, Brents and Paul Stewart!"

They continued to dance the next three dances then Jan escorted her back to her seat. She thought he might leave but he pulled up a chair and edged himself between herself and Susan. Now the steel band took a break and a woman came into the arena singing calypso songs heavy on love and interspersed with risqué double meanings.

Everyone's attention seemed to be focused on the girl whilst listening for the words that touched on topical political themes, and waiting breathlessly to see how risqué she dared to be. She was singing something about unrequited love. Juliet thought it uncannily appropriate for her present state of turmoil. Her gaze slid away from the woman and rested on Reece who was half-turned away from her, watching the singer.

Then abruptly, almost as if he could feel her eyes on him, he swung his head round and she had no time to avert her gaze. His glance clashed with hers and held it for long moments. With his sudden movement, the flames from the candles fluttered wildly, and the orange glow that flickered over his face made him appear almost feral in the dimness.

Embarrassed at being caught openly studying him she offered him an uncertain smile which he did not return. His eyes slid to Jan then back to her. Seconds later the moment was passed. He turned back to the entertainment, breaking all eye contact with Juliet.

Shortly afterwards the steel band returned and people began to stand up to dance. The Carters, Alison and

Paul, and Sally and Mason all moved into the arena, leaving her with Reece and Jan.

Excitement began to pound through Juliet's veins and she willed Reece to glance across at her again and ask her to dance. The seconds passed. She began to toy with the idea of leaning across the table and saying, "Shall we do this dance?" But then Jan took hold of her hand.

"Come on. Everyone's up. There's going to be no room left."

Juliet's hopes were dashed. She did not want to spend the rest of the evening dancing with Jan although this was obviously his intention. Except for a brush-off which would hurt him and which she could not bring herself to do, it seemed she was stuck with him for the remainder of the evening. Frustration flooded through her and she found herself impatient for each dance to end.

When they finally left the arena only Sally was sitting at the table. Jan asked her if she would like a drink. Sally told him she would really enjoy a long drink of iced lemonade. Juliet said she would have the same and Jan moved away towards the bar.

"I'm on an alcohol-free diet at the moment," Sally explained. "Doctor's orders."

Juliet was immediately full of concern. "Have you been ill?"

"Not at all. This no alcohol thing is just one of many diets Mason and I have been on in our attempts to conceive. I know it might sound faddy to you but we're so desperate to have a baby we'll try just about anything."

"Reece told me you and Mason were having difficulties."

"Difficulties! You wouldn't think that making a baby was so hard. We've tried just about everything from abstaining to yoga. This no-alcohol regime has been advised by a clinic we visited in Florida. It hasn't worked so far and I don't think it will."

"I'm so sorry," Juliet sympathized.

"I can't even begin to imagine what it must be like to want a child so badly."

Despite her despair Sally smiled and squeezed Juliet's hand. "I hope you never have to," she said generously. "I hope you have all the babies you want." She glanced away over to the bar where Jan was waiting to be served. "You seem on very friendly terms with him."

"Jan? Yes, he's really quite nice. I have underwater diving lessons with him."

"Do you know him very well?"

"Not really."

"Then take care. He has a reputation with the women who frequent the hotel. Especially the older, wealthy American guests."

"Yes, I believe so. What I can't understand is that if he has this reputation why does Reece still keep him on?"

"Reece is a shrewd businessman. As long as Jan is discreet and there are

175

no complaints why would Reece want to sack a good sports coach like Jan. And he is good. One or two come to the Island Cove to learn how to dive, most come solely to be courted by Jan, and flattered and pandered to. It gives me the creeps. After all he's only twenty-five and some of these women are approaching seventy."

"Well, I'm not wealthy, nor am I seventy, nor am I American. So according to the law of averages I should be quite safe."

Sally shrugged. "Have you thought he might have other ideas about you? Maybe something along more permanent lines?"

Juliet had to admit it hadn't crossed her mind, and Sally's words brought new confusing thoughts to play on her emotions.

"Anyway," Sally went on, "how's the diving coming along?"

Juliet looked up, pushing away her riotous thoughts. "Jan's very pleased. He thinks I'm a natural. He's already taken me into the sea. I can't wait to dive down amongst the reefs."

Sally studied the younger woman for a moment then said, "Reece is taking Mason and me out in *Razzmatazz* on Wednesday. We're going diving. Would you like to come along with us? We're all experienced divers so you wouldn't come to harm."

Juliet's eyes lit up and she had hardly had time to think about it when Reece escorted his mother back to her place.

"About Wednesday." Sally addressed her brother in a prompting tone.

"Wednesday." He puckered his lips as if in deep thought. "Ah, yes, Wednesday. I know now. It comes between Tuesday and Thursday," he teased affectionately, sitting down and leaning both arms on the table in front of him.

Sally made a face at him. "How about us taking Juliet along with us? She hasn't dived yet. Not properly anyway. She could try a little test run. Down amongst the reefs."

Juliet watched his glance slide to her and study her for a moment in silence. Then a half-smile lifted the corners of his mouth and his eyes glittered in the light from the candles.

"I once said I would never go in a boat with you again," he reminded her, his voice low and quiet so that only she could hear.

She swallowed and met his gaze boldly. "And I said it wouldn't bother me one little bit."

His mouth tilted in that wry and provocative way that caused such delightful tremors to shiver through her. "How far down have you dived?"

"Ten feet."

Now in pensive thought he twisted his mouth to one side, spoiling the sensual shape. "You can hardly call that diving."

"It's not bad in two lessons," she countered, defending her obvious inexperience. "And if I can dive to ten feet I can surely go to twenty."

Reece allowed another moment of silence to lapse. "All right," he said eventually. "But nothing more than twenty feet. And you stick close to me. No wandering off on your own. We're leaving the jetty about 10 a.m."

"That's fine." Juliet experienced a welling of excitement at the prospect of diving amongst the coral reefs. "What about diving equipment? What should I bring?"

But Juliet's enthusiastic questions were lost on Reece. Someone had called his name and glancing around Juliet saw Koelle hurrying towards the table. Good to her word, her duties being over she had arrived at the Island Cove in order to spend what was left of the evening with Reece.

Juliet's heart dropped like a stone. Watching the two of them retreat onto the dance floor she knew that he was going to dance exclusively with Koelle for the rest of the evening and she saw all hopes of feeling Reece's arms about

179

her in a close dance recede.

Of course Koelle was quite stunningly attractive, poised, and experienced in her work. Compared with her, Juliet was a plain and clumsy beginner. The American girl oozed charm to the holidaymakers in her care, and her easy-going manner seemed to go down well with all who met her. Juliet was more passionate about her work, and angry because Reece didn't seem to recognize her good points nor the hard work she was putting into her job.

Averting her eyes from the two of them she stared down at the glass of lemonade Jan had just brought from the bar, her finger tracing a bead of water as it slid down through the condensation on the outside of the glass.

"Men!" Sally snorted, and putting her hand on Juliet's arm she squeezed it sympathetically.

Glancing up Juliet was almost surprised to meet the same shrewd look in Sally's eye as the one Reece had bestowed on her so many times.

"Just bring yourself, Juliet," Sally told her quietly. "And leave everything else to us."

9

JULIET had to wait several minutes for Jan to turn up at her next lesson. He arrived at the run about 7.20 a.m. without any equipment.

"Sorry I'm late," he grunted. "I overslept."

"No problem," she said, rolling to her feet from the warm sand. "Are you all right?"

"Got a bit of a headache, that's all."

"Oh, dear." Juliet was immediately concerned for his welfare. "I understand if you don't want to dive," she told him, hoping the disappointment was not obvious in her voice.

A smile skipped across his face. "You've come all prepared."

"I was hoping we could have dived deeper today. To about twenty feet."

The smile faded and he eyed her

carefully. "What's the rush?"

"I've been invited to go diving off the reefs with Reece Carter, his sister and brother-in-law, and I'd really like to go down as far as I dare with my limited knowledge."

"To the reefs?" A sudden look of hostility came into his eyes and one so intense that Juliet recoiled. "You aren't experienced enough yet."

"Reece will stay with me," she explained.

Jan flopped down on the sand, clasped his arms around his knees and stared moodily out to sea. Juliet was alarmed by this uncharacteristic behaviour and knelt down by his side.

"I will take care."

"That's not the point," he countered grimly. "You still haven't mastered breathing through the tube. And how would you know what to do if a shark or something attacked you?"

Juliet drew back, eyes widening. "A shark?"

"Yes, a shark," he repeated. "You're

183

not on Blackpool sands now, you know. Sharks, Portuguese men o' war, octopus, Moray eels . . . the list is endless."

Juliet curled her legs beneath her and sank down. With her finger she began to trace patterns in the sand. "Is anything else the matter, Jan, apart from your headache?" she queried.

"No, everything's fine," he snapped. "Just fine."

"Are you going to give me a lesson then?" she asked quietly.

"No, no lesson today."

Juliet sat immobile for a moment, stunned and hurt by this new, terse side to Jan. Suddenly she rose to her feet. "Then there's really no point in my staying here."

Jan looked up now, all hostility receding. "No, Juliet, don't go. Look, I'm sorry if I snapped at you. It's just that . . . well, I wanted it to be me who shared your first experience down amongst the coral reefs."

That pulled Juliet up with a jerk and

she felt a sense of guilt wash over her. She had never realized until now how seriously Jan looked upon these diving lessons, and it had never crossed her mind that he would want to be the first to take her to the reefs.

"Oh, Jan, I'm sorry. I didn't realize. I didn't think . . . "

"Look . . . " He took hold of her hand, drew her back down onto the sand and swivelled round to face her. "You know what kind of man I am. I've tried to explain it to you. And then there are rumours circulating . . . "

"Yes, I've heard them. But I've passed no judgement."

"Oh, Juliet . . . " A smile lit up his sombre face. "Always so diplomatic. But I know you're not stupid, and you know there's no smoke without fire. This headache, for instance. It's because I over-indulged in alcohol last night."

"What made you do that?"

He shrugged. "My way of life, I suppose. I'm known as the hotel gigolo,

185

but whatever the rumours say, Juliet, I don't sleep with the women. I do have some pride."

Two laughing, screaming children ran down the beach and splashed into the sea. They gave Juliet an opportunity to avoid Jan's eyes. She hoped he wouldn't go into too much detail about his bizarre lifestyle at the Island Cove Hotel.

"You're the first woman I've met who isn't interested solely in me, but in the sporting knowledge I have to offer. During the time you've been here I've grown to like you and respect you." He took hold of her hand and rubbed his thumb over the silken skin. "My feelings toward you are serious."

Now Juliet swung her gaze away from the children and back to him. A frown furrowed her brow. "Jan . . . what are you saying?"

"I guess I'm trying to tell you that I care for you an awful lot, and if you could just overlook my reputation . . . "

Juliet gasped, at a loss for words.

"You know that has never really troubled me."

"Then could we perhaps see more of each other, get to know one another better? I'd leave the drink alone, and the flirting, too, if I knew I had a woman like you behind me."

Juliet's lips came together in a straight line as she assessed this new reformed character Jan was promising to project. There were a lot of things about him she liked, and had it been elsewhere in the world she might have been able to help him . . . if it hadn't been for Reece.

Her long silence was answer enough for Jan. He lifted his muscular shoulders in a shrug, as if flinging off his disappointment. "It's all right. I understand," he said, standing up and helping her to her feet.

"Jan, it's not what you think. You're a good-hearted man, considerate and pleasant to be with, but — "

"You don't have to explain." He slung an arm amicably about her shoulders. "I'd still like us to remain friends and keep up the diving lessons. You have a natural talent for water sports, and you should have no problems going down to twenty feet. Just remember the breathing exercises and to conserve your energy."

"And what about sharks and all the other horrors you mentioned?"

He laughed now, once again his jovial self. "Reece Carter is a very experienced diver. I've been out with him a couple of times. You'll be quite safe with him."

Juliet didn't resist the pressure from his arm and walked slowly with him back up through the scented gardens, listening to his story about the time when he accompanied Reece on a diving expedition to a sunken wreck some miles north of Bermuda, and the Moray eel they met that had made a home in the hull of the ship.

It was eight o'clock when they reached the hotel. He kissed her lightly on the forehead then left her, bounding off to his first tennis lesson of the day as if their conversation had never occurred.

It was at the moment when she turned away to go back to her bungalow that she saw Reece standing on the steps of the terrace. He was watching her. How long had he been there though? Had he observed Jan and herself ambling, arms across each other's backs, through the gardens? Had he seen Jan kiss her? Amidst these clashing thoughts it suddenly registered that he was coming towards her.

"Good morning." He addressed her in a clipped, businesslike tone, and she stared up at the grim male countenance, boldly meeting his cool, grey eyes. Yet for a fraction of a second she thought she saw something infiltrate that coolness, something different, something that made her heart miss a beat.

"Hello." She faced him with an even composure, expecting him to make

189

some remark about herself and Jan, but none came.

"One of your clients is ill, Miss Hamilton."

Juliet winced, realizing she had imagined the earlier softening in his eyes. It was strictly business now, and that's why he was addressing her so formally even though there was hardly anyone about. It was also perhaps his way of showing his displeasure at finding Jan and herself together.

"Oh?" Her mind ran through the list of Ultimate Tours clients, trying to pick out the one who had come to grief. It was impossible. She turned her thoughts to ailments. They were easier to guess. A bad case of sunburn, no doubt. "Who is it?"

"Mrs Andrina Saville. The hotel doctor has been to see her and has diagnosed a stomach bug. She was due to leave today but is in no fit state. The doctor has recommended she have at least forty-eight hours' rest before flying home. Could you arrange an alternative flight for her?"

"Yes, of course. I'll go and see her and get on to it right away."

She started to move towards the hotel foyer but he took hold of her arm, detaining her. Turning round she tipped her head back, seeing a nerve twitching below his cheekbone.

"Been with Jan Peters again, this morning?"

His tone was loaded and Juliet's mouth set in stubbornness. "Yes."

There was a sudden hardening of his jaw. "Another of his private diving lessons?"

"No, not this morning. Something else." She spoke in truthful innocence so she didn't understand the tightening of his mouth. "I mentioned to him about diving on the reefs. He said I should manage twenty feet."

Reece nodded curtly, accepting Jan's professional opinion. "He seemed to monopolize your company at the floorshow."

Juliet was not prepared for that

statement. It left her floundering in a sudden whirlpool of emotions with her heart leaping about within her breast. What was Reece getting at? Was he hinting at something? That maybe had Jan not been there Reece would have asked her to dance? She remembered Alison's suggestion to test him out and acted on total impulse.

"Then why didn't you rescue me?" she challenged, her voice low.

In the silence that ensued, her passionate eyes burned into the grey piercing gaze which was raking a searching glance over her features.

"I didn't think you wanted rescuing," he replied eventually, a new husky depth to his voice. "And I didn't want to appear as if I was trying to take you away from him."

"Look — "Juliet sighed and shrugged his hand off her arm. She glanced away, breaking all eye contact. "Why does everyone seem to think that Jan and I are a pair? I like him. I get on well with him. But he isn't my type."

Two dark eyebrows lifted. "What is your type, Juliet? What type of man can break through that hard shell you're encased in?"

"I'm not encased in any shell," she answered tartly. "Anyone will tell you that."

"I see," he breathed. "You just make it easier for some, and harder for others."

The low urgency in his voice brought her head round sharply and she suddenly caught a look of what could only be termed hunger before he wiped it away. She had never seen his cool, sensuous features display such emotion before. There was a swift, hot rise of her pulse, and she suddenly felt very fragile, very vulnerable.

Moments passed. Eyes locked. The intensity of his gaze was more than she could bear. Inwardly she strained towards him, trying to assert her will on him. He read her message, and understood it too. She could tell by the glinting darkness in his eyes. But he was resisting it.

"You better go and sort out Mrs Saville," he told her, and abruptly left her on the terrace, quivering and with a primitive fire raging inside her.

Up on the first floor of the Island Cove Hotel, in her suite of rooms that overlooked the beautiful cove, Mrs Andrina Saville, overweight, sixty-five years of age and with platinum blonde hair, lay in bed, listless and debilitated after a night of sickness and diarrhoea.

"It's something I ate," she wailed to Juliet. "The hotel's cleanliness is not what it should be." She reached out to her bedside table and pulled a tissue from a box. Next to it a box of chocolates lay invitingly open. Without looking Mrs Saville took the first one that came within reach of her plump, well-manicured hand and popped it into her mouth. "Miss Hamilton, you must look into it for me. Check the kitchens. Find the source of the infection."

"Yes, of course," Juliet soothed.

"But the hotel is renowned for its cleanliness." She flicked a glance at the chocolates and the empty brandy glass next to them. "I don't think the root of the problem lies with the hotel, Mrs Saville. No one else has fallen ill."

Mrs Saville's glance was sharp and defiant in its assessment of Juliet. "Then where does the fault lie, Miss Hamilton?" she boomed imperiously. "I've caught this wretched bug from somewhere. And I haven't been out of the hotel grounds. It must have come from here. You are the representative for Ultimate Tours. You must complain on my behalf. If I was well enough I'd do it myself. Tell them it's something I ate. Probably the fresh salmon. It tasted funny."

Juliet clamped her lips together, remembering the first Ultimate commandment to be diplomatic at all times. She guessed it wasn't *something* Mrs Saville had eaten, but *everything*. She flipped over the pages on her clipboard until she found a clean sheet of paper.

"Can you tell me what else you ate yesterday?"

"Good God, I couldn't possibly, child. Not everything, anyway." But she did manage to give Juliet a brief rundown on some of the things she had eaten. The mixture was fantastic and would have made even a cast-iron stomach revolt in rebellion.

"Very well, Mrs Saville." Juliet finished her scribbling. "I'll go and see Mr Scarlet right away."

"Oh, no, my dear! No! No!" Mrs Saville now raised herself onto her elbows and shook her head adamantly. "This must be discussed with no one less than Mr Carter. After all, the reputation of his hotel is on the line."

Juliet ran her fingers back through her hair. "All right, then. Mr Carter. I'll talk it over with him. Now, about your flight home . . . "

"Tell him that seeing as it's the hotel's fault they must pay for the extra two days I'm forced to stay here," she trumpeted.

Juliet hesitated, not knowing quite where she stood on this issue. This wasn't the first time she had come across an awkward guest, but she had never in her years of representing Ultimate Tours had to deal with such an unreasonable and high-handed person as Mrs Andrina Saville. She felt she was out of her depth, not knowing what to agree to and what not to agree to.

"I'll mention that also," Juliet assured the woman, trying not to consider what Reece's reaction might be to the imperious demand. She flipped through the British Airways timetable. "There's a plane leaving Bermuda at 11.30 on Friday evening. I think I could find you a seat on that plane."

Mrs Saville waved her hand listlessly, uncaring, wanting to be done with the interview. "Oh, anything, anything."

Then she clutched at her ample stomach and pulled her knees up as the chocolate took effect. A painful spasm gripped her. Juliet turned away and walked to the other side of the room, listening to Mrs Saville groaning in agony. She noticed the brandy bottle on the occasional table and yet another box of half-eaten chocolates. On the dressing-table lay a tray with plates congealed with food from the previous night's gorging.

Juliet gritted her teeth and moved across to the door separating the bedroom from the lounge. On a chair, near a window in the lounge, Mrs Saville's purse lay open, dollar notes and coins spilling from it and onto the floor. It crossed Juliet's mind to pick up the change, push the notes back into the purse and close it up, but decided against it. The whole suite was little less than a pigsty, and it was not up to her to clean up after the tetchy woman.

After a prudent interval she returned to Mrs Saville's bedside, feeling little sympathy for the wan-faced woman but not allowing it to show in her attitude.

"Would you like me to ring maid service and ask the maid to clean your room for you?"

"No," she groaned. "I don't want anyone here." She waved Juliet away. "Just go away and leave me. Let me die in peace. And don't forget to speak to Mr Carter."

Juliet didn't wait around. She didn't trust her tongue. Hurrying from the room she stood for a moment in the corridor outside, wallowing in its light airiness after the stuffy darkness of Mrs Saville's sickroom.

Right away she got on with the job of seating Mrs Saville on Friday night's plane which she managed without a problem. Then she went to see Reece Carter. He was sitting with his back to the desk, his elbows on the arm rests, his fingertips pressed together as he stared out of the window, unheedful of the untouched paperwork that lay scattered across the desktop behind him.

"Have you a moment?" she asked,

breaking the silence in the room.

He swivelled round in his chair and rolled to his feet, fixing her with a long, speculative gaze.

"Juliet," he said quietly, uncertainly.

"Yes, of course. You look harassed."

"I am."

Closing the door behind her she walked across to the desk and without invitation slammed her file and clipboard down on the leather surface, every movement indicative of intense irritation. Reece blinked as if coming out of a stupor, glanced down at the abruptly deposited pile, then raised his eyes questioningly to her.

"Mrs Saville," she informed him tartly.

"Ah . . . yes." Reece pulled his mouth into a tight line. "Mrs — Andrina — Saville." He spoke slowly and with deliberation, putting much emphasis on each name. "Have you managed to sort anything out?"

"Yes, the best bit. The flight home," Juliet retorted acidly. "She is adamant that her stomach upset is the fault of the hotel."

"Is she now!" There was a slight tilt to his mouth which suggested he had lived through such accusations before. "What do *you* think, Juliet?"

"Me?" She uttered a half laugh. "I think it's her own fault for eating too much rich food yesterday. You should see her room, Reece. It's in a mess and she refuses to call maid service. Even now she's gorging herself on chocolates. And look . . . " Juliet picked up the clipboard, flipped over the sheets of paper until she found the salient one, and presented it to him. "This is a list of some of the things — only some, mind you — that she ate yesterday. And she instructed me to tell you that the fresh salmon tasted funny."

Reece's mouth quirked in that wry, familiar way as he ran an eye down the list, but he said nothing.

"And what's more," Juliet added, miffed, "she is also demanding that the hotel pay for the extra two days she's having to spend here."

"Yes, well I expected that." Reece handed the clipboard back to her. "It will be arranged."

Juliet almost dropped the board. She went to catch it, disrupting some of the neatly clipped papers. "You mean you're agreeing to her demands?"

"Yes."

"But Reece," she protested, "she's a dreadful woman."

"That may be. But she is a guest — however dreadful. Mrs Saville comes here faithfully every year for a month at a time, and every year she eats too much rich food, drinks too much brandy, and falls ill, blaming it all on badly prepared food in ill-equipped kitchens. This isn't the first time, nor will it be the last, that the hotel has given her extra days free of charge."

"What a con!" Juliet exclaimed.

"In our favour, though," Reece countered. "She pays almost two thousand pounds sterling a week for the best suite in the hotel. And that doesn't include food. What with her bar bill and other extras it all adds up to about ten thousand pounds for the month. On the other hand, it costs us maybe one hundred pounds — probably less — to pander to her whims for a couple of extra days. It's called business."

His mouth curved into a fascinating smile that suddenly exploded into sheer dynamite. Acutely unnerved Juliet's mind was wiped clean of everything. She forgot Mrs Saville, her illness, her imperious attitude that had got Juliet's back up. All composure deserted her as she became ensnared in that tantalizing smile.

With an effort she tried to pull herself together, but it wasn't enough. No longer able to project the chatty, flowing, easy manner she had adopted with him she fumbled for her file and turned to go.

"I don't think I could ever be a business woman," she murmured for something to say.

Reece accompanied her to the door, opening it for her. "Everyone to their own."

She smiled up at him, nervousness causing a fine sheen of perspiration to erupt over her body, then made to leave the office, but her way became suddenly barred as he thrust out an arm, pressing his hand against the opposite door jamb.

"You've shown that you can execute your own job admirably. I think I should tell you there has been much praise from guests regarding your helpful manner." His gaze drifted over her like a feather caressing each feature. "I'm pleased to have you with us."

"Does . . . " She stumbled over her words, her voice low. "Does that mean I'm no longer under observation?"

"Not by the hotel," he replied obliquely, and dropped his arm, allowing her to pass through.

10

ON the Wednesday morning Juliet arrived at the jetty a little before ten o'clock. It was promising to be hot that day. The temperature was already nudging the nineties. She had chosen to wear a pair of multicoloured striped shorts and a white cotton T-shirt with insets in the sleeves of the same material as her shorts. She had a pair of canvas deck shoes on her feet and carried her swimming costume and a change of clothes in a canvas bag which she slung over her shoulder. Her thick, long chestnut hair she had tied back into a ponytail then plaited.

Sally and Mason were already loading *Razzmatazz* and welcomed her warmly. "Lordie, isn't it hot?" Sally observed. "I'm glad we're not staying here today. It's going to be overbearing."

"Can you pass me those masks by your feet?" Mason asked Juliet. "Then I think we have everything."

"Everything except the captain," Sally put in, taking the masks from Juliet. "You haven't seen him, have you?"

"Reece? No . . ."

Sally sighed impatiently. "Where has that brother of mine got to?"

"He's coming," Mason put in and Juliet swung round, watching the man who was devastating her normally placid life.

He walked along the jetty in a brisk way that suggested he was aware of his lateness, wearing a blue chambray shirt and shorts, and carrying a cool-box. Juliet decided that whatever it was that made a woman lose sight of her reasoning, Reece Carter had it.

As he approached the boat he slowed down. Juliet's gaze ran over his lazy smile of greeting without being able to judge anything from it. But in his all-encompassing glance she read the awareness that the shape of her body appealed to him.

"You're late!" Chiding, Sally cut through the magnetism that was building up. She reached out and took the cool-box from him. "We were beginning to think you weren't coming."

"Sorry," Reece apologized. "Couldn't find a bottle opener for the wine."

He turned back to Juliet offering her a hand to step from the jetty onto the diving platform at the stern, then into the cockpit, striding in after her. They stored all the gear to the rear of the driver-station with its custom-designed seat and dash, then Sally and Juliet went below to take down the cool-box.

The cabin was ultra modern, decorated in scarlet, white and soft grey. To one side there was a small kitchen fully equipped with microwave oven, fridge and sink. On the other side there was a shower with both hot and cold running water supplied from a fresh water system. The rest of the cabin was taken up by bulkhead seats in grey with scarlet scatter cushions, and tailing off into the V of the bow was a double bed. The lighting was soft and subdued and miniature Venetian blinds covered each rectangular-shaped portlight.

Up in the cockpit Reece and Mason had already cast off. The engine was purring, just ticking over as the bow inched forward away from the jetty and sailed like a sedate old steamer out into the bay.

Only when the beach was left far behind did Reece pull out the throttle. Then the engine burst into roaring life. The stern sank down, the bow lifted and the boat sprang forward, the sudden force of gravity pinning everyone back against their seats.

Juliet took a deep breath, exulting in the tangy freshness of the air and the sudden force of the cooling breeze as it rushed past. Skimming the waves and feeling the spray from the water displaced by the bows Juliet could not remember ever feeling so good, so alive. It was as if she were a child again and playing out the dreams of youth.

An hour later they had left the islands of Bermuda well behind and were skimming across the dark blue ocean towards a hump on the horizon that grew rapidly as the boat shot towards it. Reece throttled back, turned towards the island shore and slowed to a speed just below idle. Breaking waves pinpointed a reef.

"How much does she draw?" Mason asked.

"About three and a half feet," Reece told him. "We should get through with no trouble. Keep a look out, will you?"

Mason clambered over the hull of the boat whilst Juliet listened to the low purr of the engine. They found a niche in the reef where the boat could squeeze through, crossed the first line of rocks, then the second. Reece backed the boat round until the stern faced the shore, turned off the engine and let the boat drift until it finally settled, nearly motionless, about ten yards from the tropical, coral-pink beach. Reece proposed that they should dive before eating.

"But I'm dying of hunger," wailed Mason, patting his stomach.

"Me, too," added Sally. "It must be the sea air. Let's eat first."

Reece however was adamant that it was bad practice to eat before diving so they followed his advice, donned tanks and masks and slipped overboard.

Juliet noticed that about his waist Reece wore a belt with a sheath attached to it on his right side. From the top jutted the bone handle of a knife. It reminded her that they were not off the coast of Britain, but in semi-tropical waters where all kinds of dangers lurked unheeded by the inexperienced diver.

The four of them separated. Mason and Sally swam away, diving expertly to the deeper waters away from the reef. Reece tapped Juliet on the shoulder and indicated the strap around her waist that held the oxygen tank in place and which she had forgotten to tie. She secured it. He put up thumb and index finger together in the universal okay sign then beckoned for her to stay with him. She nodded and followed close behind as he swam deeper below the surface.

The water was crystal clear, aiding the vertical rainbow shafts of sunlight as it filtered down, bringing out all the natural colours on the reef.

It was a virtually silent world down there. The only noises were the soft whistle as she inhaled and a bubbly rattle as she exhaled. Behind her mask Juliet's eyes widened as she studied at close hand the giant sea-anemones and watched the darting fish, alarmed by Reece's and her arrival on their territory.

Rocks rose up before them, and beyond, the water took on a darker, more mysterious hue, almost sinister.

They passed by a piece of coral, its smooth, mustard-coloured surface inviting touch. Juliet put out her hand. Reece grasped it and yanked it away, slipping a protective arm about her waist and drawing her close to him. He pointed to the coral and shook his head, warning her away. Then he made a motion as if he had been burned. Juliet nodded, understanding. Reece took hold of her hand and led her away, giving the fire-coral a wide berth.

How long they stayed under swimming close together, sometimes hands linked, Juliet had no idea, but by the time they surfaced she needed help in staggering ashore and taking off her tank.

"I'm so tired," she admitted, surprised at her lack of energy.

"Because you're not an experienced diver." He untied the straps of the tank and slid it from her back. "What did you think?"

"Oh, Reece," she sighed, "I've never experienced anything like it. The colours, the light, the fish . . . I just want to go back down and have another look."

"Not today," he advised. "You've done enough for one day."

She took the towel he offered her and gave herself a quick rub down. Then she reached up and tried to untie her wet hair, but strands of it had become entangled with the bands, causing her to grimace as she tried to drag them out.

"Here, let me do that," Reece volunteered. Standing behind her he was able to see what had happened and quickly resolved the matter, freeing her hair from the restraining bands.

Heavy with sea-water her hair fell down in rich, chestnut waves, draping over her shoulders and forming fronds about her cheeks and forehead. He took the towel from about his neck and starting at her cheekbones he drew back her hair, gently squeezing the water from it. There was a certain sensuality in his touch. It burned her like fire. She stepped away and turned round to face him.

"How long were we down?"

His gaze was sweeping over the moisture beading on her bare shoulders. "How long do you think?"

"Hours probably."

He raised his eyes to study her, a smile slanting his mouth. "Forty minutes, actually. Long enough."

Tossing the towel to her he hunkered down on his haunches and began to unpack the cool-box. For a moment, as she slowly ran the towel over her hair, she studied the play of muscles across his shoulders and down the length of his brown back. Something akin to awe surfaced in her.

She dispensed with the towel and helped him to prepare the food. Mason and Sally waded ashore soon afterwards, ravenously hungry by now and ready to devour the sausages, chicken and salad. They completed their meal with fruit and chilled white wine.

Afterwards Mason waded out in the aquamarine water to where *Razzmatazz* was gently riding the swell and wandered around her hull.

"Look at him!" Sally laughed. "He's so envious he's almost the colour of the sea."

Reece returned her laugh and raised his voice so that Mason could hear above the pounding of the surf. "Want to take her for a spin?"

Mason grinned and placed both hands on his hips. "What took you so long to offer? Come on, Sal. Let's see if we can get more than seventy miles an hour out of this old bathtub."

Reece cringed. "Ruin the engine and you'll foot the bill."

Watching Sally run down the beach and leap the waves like a young schoolgirl Juliet hugged her arms about her legs and rested her chin on her knees.

"They're such a wonderful couple, Reece. I do hope they can have a child soon."

She lay back on the sand, tired, replete with food and her mind a riot of memories from the dive.

Whether she slept she couldn't be certain, but in the lethargic stupor into which she had sunk she sensed a sudden shadow, as if a cloud had passed over the sun. She opened her eyes. Reece was leaning over her, his head angled slightly to watch the way she slept. A lazy smile curved his mouth.

"Did I wake you?"

She met his eyes boldly, exhibiting no shyness. "Yes."

"Good." There was a low, husky timbre to his voice. "I've been watching you lie there for half an hour just waiting for you to wake up." His hands went to her shoulders, rubbing the sun-warmed rounded curve of her bones. "And a man can only wait so long . . . "

Juliet tingled beneath his touch and didn't even begin to consider what might follow. It seemed the most natural thing in the world to place the flat of her palms on his chest.

Her fingers felt the smoothness of his skin and the involuntary contractions of his muscles beneath. Slowly she let her hands slide up, gliding across his shoulders and around his neck. His own hands tightened over her shoulders and pulled her up so that she would meet his descending mouth halfway.

His hard, hungry kiss established dominion over her lips before mellowing into a deep and gentle passion. The kiss was laced with experience but it wasn't technique that set her primitive fires alight. It was a basic instinct in her that had gone unrequited for so long and now begged to be assuaged. So she returned it, wallowing in the wildness his embrace was bringing, pressing herself closer to him until she was satisfied she was moulded against him and able to feel the burning heat of his flesh leaving its imprint on her.

When his mouth dropped to the hollow of her throat and began nibbling the curve of her neck she couldn't contain the soft, quivering sound that came from within her, and threw her head back, exposing the long line of her throat to his searching lips.

"You know" — her voice was a disturbed whisper — "I think there was an ulterior motive to your invitation to Mason to take the boat out."

His laugh was a soft and throaty growl from deep inside him as he slid the thin straps of her swimming costume from her shoulders, to enable his mouth to sample the smooth expanse of skin across her chest. "We couldn't very well have done this with Sal and Mason around, could we?"

"You schemer!" she murmured, pressing her lips to the naked skin of his shoulder, liking its smoothness and tasting the salt from the sea.

"How else could I get you completely alone?" he muttered thickly. "I've been trying hard enough for the past few days." His hand was on her waist, feeling its slenderness, testing the flare of her hips below. His other arm was beneath her shoulders, pushing her up to him. "Do you know how good this feels? You're enough to drive a man crazy."

She made some sort of agreeing sound, completely lost in his embrace, and he uttered an animal-like groan of satisfaction.

"You're bewitching, Juliet," he murmured. "Of all the women — glamorous, wealthy, beautiful — who have passed through the hotel, not one has been quite like you." He pushed her down onto the sand and leaned over, his body half-covering hers. "I took your advice." His mouth travelled up to her ear, gently nibbling and tugging the lobe whilst his hand moved up from her waist and brushed over the rounded curve of her breast.

"Oh?" she gasped breathlessly. If his touch became more intimate she doubted she would have the willpower to stop him. "What advice is that?"

"The villa," he murmured throatily. "I've bought it."

Juliet froze. The moment of intense

passion was broken. With those few words he had reminded her of Koelle. Unintentionally, of course. Well on the way to dizzy heights himself he would have had no wish to bring to an end the warm, cloying desire that was encapsulating the two of them.

She felt unsure of herself and of him. At that moment he had raised a sharp feeling of resentment in her. What was his game? And what of Koelle Wiseman?

Placing her hands on his shoulders she pushed him off, rolled out from under him and sprang to her feet, missing already the strength of his arms about her.

Pulling the straps of her swimming costume back over her shoulders she ran down the beach and into the sea, putting distance between herself and Reece. Thoughts were swirling around her head in such confusion that she had no sense of location or direction.

When the pain struck her foot it was total, all-encompassing, wiping everything from her anguished mind. She cried out as she collapsed into the shallow water and grabbed her foot, turning it over to find the source of the pain.

Seeing her fall, Reece rolled to his feet and ran after her into the sea. "Juliet, what's the matter?"

"I don't know." The words came out on a tight little gasp. "My foot. It hurts."

"Where?" He knelt down in the sun-warmed surf and took her foot in his hand.

"Underneath," she told him. "On the heel."

He ran an expert eye over the underside of her foot but the waves kept buffeting them, making it difficult for him to make a diagnosis.

"I think you might have stepped on a sea-urchin."

"It felt more like a pin-cushion."

He grunted. "There's little difference. Let's get you back to the beach."

He bent to help her but she shrugged

him off, suddenly remembering the reason why she had run from him into the water.

"I can manage on my own!"

"I'd like to see you try." Without further argument he swept her, protesting, into his arms and carried her back up the sand.

"Will you put me down, for Heaven's sake!" she snapped. "I'm not an invalid."

He did so, depositing her with little grace onto the sand. "What on earth made you get up and run off like that?"

There was a ragged edge of anger to his voice. Juliet didn't reply and lay back on her elbows, grimacing whilst he raised her foot and studied it again. A small string of profanities erupted from him, proving he possessed a sound knowledge of basic Anglo-Saxon.

"The spines are embedded. I'll have to get them out. Christ, Juliet, this would never have happened if you hadn't taken off like that."

"I wouldn't have run off if you hadn't forced yourself on me. *Ow!*"

Reece was in the process of pulling out the tiny spines one by one, but he paused and glanced up, his narrowed eyes flashing like steel in the sunlight.

"I don't recall forcing myself on you. In fact, if my memory serves me right, it was you who made the first move. Remember?"

Juliet withered beneath his unrelenting stare and looked away, biting on her bottom lip to suppress the yelp of pain surging up in her. She was convinced she would never walk again, and began to consider the distinct possibility that she might die before nightfall.

Reece now had his mouth pressed to the heel of her foot, sucking, teeth searching and pulling out the spines.

"You know" — there was a sudden edge of wickedness to his voice — "in other circumstances this would be a highly erotic experience."

Her glance swung back to him, taking

in the amused glint in his eyes. "Not funny, Reece!" she snapped. "You're mad!"

"I know." He spat one of the spines into the sand. "I think I'm losing my head."

"What?" She lifted her pain-pinched face so that she could see him better. His mouth was quirking in the way that always intrigued her.

"I'm getting turned on just dragging these damned things out of your foot with my teeth. Has anyone ever told you what a beautiful foot you've got?"

Juliet flopped back onto the sand and closed her eyes. She knew that the rounded contours of her body sang to him and excited his male instincts, but she despised him for flirting with her so freely and discussing the intimate state of his feeling when he had just told her he had bought the villa — a beautiful, Bermudan residence that he would share with another woman.

She wrenched her foot from out of

his grasp and sat up, curling her legs under her. She didn't know which was worse — the sharp pain in her foot or the ache of unrequited love inside her. There and then she made up her mind that the intimate moments they had shared was a mistake she didn't intend to repeat.

On the return sea journey Juliet lay on the big double bed. Sally managed to extract several more spines with a pair of eyebrow tweezers she kept in her bag whilst Mason navigated and Reece watched the delicate operation in brooding silence, his dark gaze still reflecting the passion she had raised in him.

Juliet's anger had melted away as quickly as it had arisen. Looking into his eyes and seeing the want still hovering there she realized she was kidding herself about avoiding him in the future. In those moments of raw passion a threshold had been crossed and she knew that she would not be able to stop herself from re-crossing it any time the opportunity presented itself.

She was also all too aware that her sudden and unexplained rejection of him had hit him hard and had been a slap to his manhood. She wanted to hold out her arms to him and make up. But what good would that do except draw a temporary veil over the matter? She looked away from his dark, brooding gaze and closed her eyes. In her mind she was back in his arms. She could hear the rasp of his breath, feel the male build of his body that incited her basic instincts. She began to feel dizzy.

"God, Reece, are you sure those spines weren't poisonous?" Sally's anxious voice cut through the images Juliet was trying to block from her mind. "She's come over all flushed and hot."

"They weren't poisonous." His voice was tight with confusion and suppressed anger. "It was just a simple sea-urchin, that's all."

His motionless stance was broken by

a surge of energy, and swinging round he climbed the stairs back into the cockpit. Sally watched him go, then turned back.

"I'm sorry," Juliet apologized, trying to make some excuse for his abrupt behaviour. "Reece is angry because I've spoiled your day."

"Don't be silly." Sally put out her hand and squeezed Juliet's arm. "Reece is irritated, yes. But not because of the accident." And she fixed shrewd eyes on Juliet, eyes that saw so much but gave little away.

For a moment she waited, offering Juliet an opening to explain what had happened, but Juliet shook her head and turned her face to the bulkhead, summoning up memories even though she knew they would torture her very soul.

She recalled the desire that had flooded through both hers and Reece's bodies on the sand. They had experienced a need that could well have been consummated if she hadn't run from him, and she was suddenly tormented by images of Reece in the arms of the American girl. He would for sure go to her that night, and she would fulfil that which Juliet had failed to do.

Automatically she raised her hand and caressed her lips with the tips of her fingers.

11

THE next day Juliet's heel was so sore and inflamed that she could hardly walk except by hobbling on the ball of her foot. The doctor had removed all the spines and given her some spray lotion that froze her foot for a time, eased the pain and reduced the inflammation.

Just after lunch the phone in her bungalow rang and reception advised her that Mr Carter wanted to see her as soon as possible.

Juliet slammed down the receiver, irritated and angry that Reece should be making her walk all the way to the hotel in her condition. He was well aware of her painful injury so what was he playing at?

She slipped out of her shorts and into her regulation dress, put on her most comfortable pair of sandals and limped slowly along the meandering paths to the main building.

Juliet was bemused to find that Reece's secretary appeared much cooler towards her. In fact her attitude was brusque and very business-like when she told Juliet to go right in.

On entering Reece's office she was surprised to find Alan Scarlet sitting to one side of the room; and most disconcerting of all was the presence of Mrs Andrina Saville, who sat smoking a cigarette from a long holder and who looked fit, healthy and bronzed after her two extra days at the hotel's expense.

"Ah, Miss Hamilton." Reece stood up and put out a hand, indicating a vacant chair that had been placed ominously in front of his desk. "Come in and sit down. How's your foot today?"

"Sore and very swollen," she told him.

Juliet ran an assessing glance over his face but his features were set in an impenetrable mask that revealed nothing, and which certainly showed no indication of what had passed between them the previous day. She sat down in silence.

"I apologize for bringing you over here with your injury but I'm afraid it's necessary," Reece explained.

He paused now, glanced down at his desk and made an unnecessary adjustment to the angle of his pen lying on the blotter. He seemed reluctant to continue and cleared his voice, as if playing for time. Juliet felt a stab of alarm pierce her. She had never seen indecision in him before.

"This isn't very pleasant for me, Miss Hamilton," Reece began, raising his eyes and meeting her bemused gaze. "On Tuesday Mrs Saville fell ill and you went along to her room to see if she needed anything. Is that right?"

Juliet stared at him and gave a small nervous laugh. "Yes, you know it is."

He didn't return her laugh. All traces of the warmth she had seen yesterday were missing from his features, and his face remained a sombre mask which set her pulse racing madly.

"How long did you stay with her?"

Juliet shrugged. "Maybe twenty minutes. I can't be sure."

"And in that time," Reece went on, "did you leave her bedside?"

"Yes. She was suffering from a spasm of pain so I walked away so that she could have a little privacy."

"Where did you go?" Reece queried.

An uneasy prickling sensation coursed through her at his official line of questioning. "I — I — don't know." Confusion clouded her thinking. "To the window, perhaps. No, I remember now. I went to the door of the bedroom, the one leading into the lounge."

"Did anyone else come into the suite whilst you were there?"

"No, I was alone with Mrs Saville."

There was a slight pause whilst Reece fidgeted with the cuff of his shirt. "Miss Hamilton — " his tone lowered and Juliet thought that just for a flash of a moment there was something akin to torment in his eyes — "did you see Mrs Saville's evening purse?"

"Yes," she replied without hesitation. "It was lying open on an occasional table."

"Was there any money in it?"

"I don't know whether there was any money actually in it. But there were certainly some notes lying on the table top and some had fallen onto the floor." All of a sudden Juliet lost patience. "Mr Carter, what is this all about?"

"This morning, Mrs Saville went to pack her suitcase and noticed some money was missing from her evening purse." He paused again. Juliet noticed a muscle working in his cheek. When he spoke again it was with a degree of reluctance. "Mrs Saville has accused you of taking twenty dollars from her purse."

Total silence fell on the room. Juliet's mouth dropped open. Stupefied she stared at Reece, her widening gaze locked on him. Her face paled. She lost all powers of speech.

"Juliet." Reece's voice was sharp to break the spell that held her.

She jumped, then blinked. Colour returned to her face in a rush of angry pink. "It's not true," she cried out. "I've never stolen anything in my life." She almost choked on her bitter words.

"But of course she'd say that," trumpeted Mrs Saville, leaning forward and stubbing out her cigarette in the ashtray. She sat back, her superior and arrogant eyes settling on the young girl. "Anybody in her shoes would lie about seeing the money."

With a sudden and completely unexpected surge of energy Reece swung round. "Mrs Saville," he stated coolly, "may I remind you that Miss Hamilton has not denied seeing the money falling from your purse."

Mrs Saville puffed up her large body and clamped her mouth shut. Reece turned back to Juliet. His eyes were brilliant now with some powerful emotion that refused to be checked.

"When you saw the money what did you do?"

"How do you mean?" Juliet queried, wary now of what to say in case she incriminated herself in some way.

"Did you touch it?" Reece suggested. "Or pick it up off the floor, perhaps, and replace it on the table?"

The beat of Juliet's heart merged from rapid strokes to long, thick thuds that made her feel light-headed. Her mouth became tacky. "The thought did cross my mind but I left it."

"Why?" queried Reece.

Juliet saw her chance to ease suspicion from herself and shift it to the careless and negligent Mrs Saville. "Because both rooms were in such a dreadfully untidy state anyway that me picking up a few dollar notes wouldn't have made any impression."

Mrs Saville shot forward in her chair, clearly incensed that a lowly employee should have the temerity to pass an oblique comment upon her character. Her eyes shot daggers at Juliet.

"I have been coming here for the past fifteen years, and never, in all that time has anyone ever spoken to me like that." She swung back to Reece. "The tone of your hotel is lowering, Mr Carter, and will continue to do so whilst you employ rude young women like this. I think you should terminate her employment here."

"Miss Hamilton is not employed by me so I can't do that," he replied levelly.

Mrs Saville's eyes narrowed. "Can't or won't, Mr Carter? It's clear you're doubting my word."

"Mrs Saville, I'm taking no sides." Reece spoke quietly but firmly. "This is a delicate and very unpleasant situation."

"I don't like it any more than you do," she retorted. "But you might at least have the decency to come down on my side. Isn't the paying guest always right?"

The emphasis on the word 'paying' was lost on no one. Reece pulled his mouth into a tight line. Juliet could almost read what was going through his mind. The word of Mrs Saville, a wealthy guest who paid thousands of pounds into his coffers? Or that of Juliet, a mere holiday rep with a propensity for speaking her mind and upsetting the smooth running of his exalted hotel?

The silence that followed was more vocal than any words. Juliet stared up into his grim face, hurt and resentful beyond belief. Was he really considering sacrificing her to maintain the reputation of his hotel and to keep Andrina Saville as a client? Even though he must surely know Juliet was innocent? Even though they had shared such intimate moments the previous day?

Alan Scarlet's timely cough cut through Juliet's distress and indicated that he wished to speak. Reece glanced across at him.

"I think we might be able to sort this out, Mr Carter. In my office with Mrs Saville."

"You have some constructive observation?" Reece demanded, making no effort now to disguise the sheer irritation flowing through him.

Alan Scarlet did not waver beneath the snappish tone. "Yes, I think I have."

"Very well." Reece turned back to Juliet. "Wait here, would you, Miss Hamilton?"

The three of them left the room leaving Juliet alone to stare, mortified, out of the window. Even in her distraught state she noticed Luke, the old, retired gardener, making a feeble effort at hoeing the dry soil.

The large hand of time moved silently as Juliet's fate was discussed in low murmurs in the next office. She didn't want to hear what was being said so she concentrated on Luke and continued to follow his lethargic movements, feeling like an accused person in a courtroom awaiting a verdict. There and then she made a resolve that whatever the outcome, she would have to leave the hotel and put in for a transfer.

After a considerable time Reece returned alone. Juliet searched his face for some sign of encouragement but his features were set in a cold, hostile expression. She withered in her seat. Reece moved across to the desk and perched in front of her, studying her carefully.

"You'll be pleased to learn that everything's been resolved."

"Resolved?" she repeated, her heart leaping, her spirits bursting with hope. "What do you mean? Has Mrs Saville admitted her mistake?"

"No. It all means that the hotel will reimburse the twenty dollars Mrs Saville claims is missing from her purse."

The surge of hope was immediately cancelled. "Reimburse her!" Juliet's cry of horror cut through the quiet atmosphere of the office. "So what you're saying is that yes, I did steal the money."

"No, I'm not saying that at all. But you would be wise to accept the incident as closed."

"You mean I must forget everything?" Juliet's voice trembled.

"If you are sensible, yes. Mrs Saville was threatening to call the police . . . "

"Police! My God . . . "

"Juliet." Reece's quiet, controlled tones were in stark contrast to her own frantic voice. "It was done for your own good as well as that of the hotel. She is prepared to forget what happened."

Indignation soared in her but she fought to get herself under control and lowered her voice. "Forget? Well, not me!" She stood up now, her face on a level with his. Unmindful of her injured heel she put her weight on it. The pain shot through her foot and up her leg, causing her to stumble. Reece reached out and steadied her.

"Juliet, take it easy."

"How can I take it easy?" Her voice trembled and the mute appeal in her eyes quickly reached out to Reece. "Don't you understand how humiliating all this is for me?"

"I can imagine." He gathered her gently in his arms, pulled her between his legs and let her press her forehead against the solidness of his shoulder.

"She accused me of stealing money from her purse, Reece. My name has not been cleared. I'm still a thief both in her eyes and in yours."

"Juliet, don't be ridiculous," he murmured.

He rubbed his hand comfortingly over her back, and moved his jaw to and fro over the silken chestnut hair. Juliet knew his intention was to comfort her, but even in her distress she became acutely aware of his hands exploring the womanly contours of her shape. It evoked the desires he had awoken in her the previous day. She moved away from his arms and Reece let her go.

"It's not worth getting upset for twenty wretched dollars, Juliet," he reasoned.

She uttered a bitter laugh. "It's not you who's been accused. Oh, to be rich!" she declaimed. "To accuse someone of stealing, then play the role of the magnanimous forgiver and condescend to let them off."

With a sigh Reece stood up, moved across to a cabinet and opened it to reveal several bottles of spirits. Unscrewing a bottle of brandy he poured a small amount into a glass and handed it to her. But she waved it aside angrily.

"I don't want a drink, Reece. I want my name cleared."

"I don't know how I can do that," Reece replied gently, setting down the glass. "Mrs Saville is perhaps careless, a little forgetful. Maybe she counted her money wrongly. Or maybe she thought she had more than she actually had. That's the only comfort I can offer you. She'll be leaving this evening and then the whole unfortunate episode will be forgotten."

"But I won't be able to forget, Reece. Ever. Don't you understand? My name has been sullied, my character brought into disrepute." Tears of hurt and humiliation sprang to her eyes. "Can't you see that?" She stopped, half choking. She was on the verge of crying.

"For the love of God!" Reece was moving towards her again but her pride and dignity would not allow him to see her break down completely. She spun on her good heel, knowing what she had to do.

"Juliet." The low urgency of his voice made her stop briefly and look back over her shoulder. A muscle was working along his jawline. "Juliet, don't go. Let's clear this between us."

Already the tears were overflowing down her cheeks. She shook her head and opened the door before he reached her, touched her, and she succumbed to a pitiful display of weeping.

She left his office as quickly as her painful foot would allow. She was halfway across the spacious reception area when the automatic doors slid open from the gardens and Sally walked in.

"Hello, Juliet. I've just been over to your bungalow to see how you are." As she approached and saw Juliet's crumpling face her step faltered. "Dear Lord, what's happened? Are you ill?" One arm automatically curled around Juliet's shoulders. "What is it?"

"Oh, Sally," Juliet sighed wearily, tormented both by her misery and the pain in her foot. "I've just come from Reece's office. One of the guests has accused me of stealing twenty dollars from her purse."

"What?" Sally stared at Juliet, assessing the hurt that such a dreadful accusation had brought. Taking her arm she helped the young girl into the lounge and ordered afternoon tea to be served at their table.

Whilst waiting for the waiter to bring

it Sally held Juliet's hand comfortingly in her own. Juliet's other hand was pressed against her mouth, her moist eyes staring blankly out of the window.

Eventually the tea was brought — silver service with delicate china cups and saucers, and eye-catching little cakes on a matching cake stand.

"So how's your foot?" Sally questioned brightly as she poured out the tea.

"Pardon?" Juliet brought herself from the depths of misery and glanced across at Sally.

"Your foot," Sally repeated. "How is it?"

"Very sore. That spray stuff the doctor gave me only works for so long and then the pain comes back. He says it will take a few days."

"Poor you!" Sally smiled sympathetically and handed her a cup of tea. "You could really have done without the aggro, couldn't you? Who accused you, anyway?"

Juliet sipped at the hot tea, feeling the immediate benefit of refreshment.

"Andrina Saville."

"Oh, that old fusspot!" To Juliet's surprise Sally dismissed the wealthy woman with a contemptuous wave of her hand. "As if she would miss twenty dollars! She could lose half a million without noticing. What had Reece got to say about it?"

A frown clouded Juliet's face. She put down her cup and saucer and gazed out of the window. "The hotel has reimbursed her the missing money, and Reece has given me the benefit of the doubt which means he's not actually sure. No one can be totally sure, can they, because there's no proof. So that accusation still lurks beneath the surface." She turned back now, her blue eyes filled with sudden torment. "Do you suppose he'll have to report all this to Ultimate Tours? They'll ask for my resignation, won't they?"

Sally popped a cake in her mouth and patted Juliet's hand. "You're letting everything get out of perspective. I suppose you can't understand why

Reece didn't come down hard on the old dear and tell her to get lost. Well, he can't do that, no matter how much he would like to. Reece has a business to run, a hotel that brings in millions of dollars a week. He has to be seen to be fair whilst being diplomatic at the same time. It's all very tricky. But he is a good judge of character, believe me. I've known him for thirty-three years. If he had believed you to be capable of being light-fingered you wouldn't be sitting here now drinking tea. You'd be packing your bags for the next flight home. Like Koelle Wiseman." She picked up the teapot. "Do you want a refill?"

Staring idly into her cup and listening to Sally's run of comforting words, it took Juliet a moment to realize just what Sally had said. As the light dawned she looked up quickly, automatically handing Sally her cup and saucer. Her own problems receded and curiosity came to the fore.

"What are you talking about?"

"Don't you know about the Koelle Wiseman fiasco? I thought it would have got around the hotel by now. She was found doing naughty things with one of the waiters."

"Naughty things?" Juliet was suddenly thrown into confusion. "What do you mean, naughty things?"

Sally's eyes widened and twinkled in delight. "Come on, Juliet. Use your imagination. You know . . . nudge, nudge, wink, wink. She's being transferred back home to Florida. I don't know whether she'll lose her job or what."

"Transferred . . . back to Florida . . . but Reece, does Reece know?"

Sally looked startled. "Reece? Why of course he knows. He's the one who sent her packing."

"But I thought he and Koelle . . . " Juliet stopped, suspecting she was about to make a fool of herself. "I thought they . . . I thought he was quite close to her."

"Well, he was, I suppose, in a way.

248

He knows her parents and promised that he'd keep an eye on her whilst she was over here. She's a bit of a wild one and everyone thought that if she got herself a nice job where she met people she'd calm down. I think Reece felt he had to try to keep her on the straight and narrow. But it's all a bit chaotic, now, with Koelle gone and you out of commission. Everything's falling on poor Alison. She'll cope, though, I know. And Exotica are sending out a replacement rep today . . . "

Juliet heard the run of Sally's voice but she was hardly listening to what she was saying. Everyone's hints at Reece's and Koelle's relationship had been well-meaning, baseless gossip. Not true facts.

If only she had had the foresight to ask Sally earlier about Koelle and Reece, the truth would have been revealed and none of the emotional trauma she had gone through the past few weeks would have occurred. She could have given herself up to developing their relationship instead of hindering it. Not that it made much difference now, anyway. With Andrina Saville's accusatory finger pointing at Juliet, and Reece hardly veiling his own suspicions, she was now obliged to leave the hotel and would never be able to work towards discovering a newer more intense relationship with him.

12

HER mind made up, Juliet thanked Sally for the tea, returned her comforting embrace and made straight for the office behind the reception desk.

The fax machine was in use. Juliet waited around for a while but the local anaesthetic was wearing off and the pain returning in her foot. She asked one of the hotel secretaries to fax her request for immediate transfer to Ultimate Tours in London, then requested that one of the messengers bring the reply to her bungalow when it eventually came through.

Juliet was sitting out on the small terrace, dressed in a black halterneck bikini, her mind constantly jumping from Andrina Saville's accusation to Sally's startling news about Koelle, when the knock came at the door.

In one way she had hoped Ultimate Tours' answer would not arrive so promptly. She had wanted so much one last time to wander, unhindered by her sore foot, around the luscious gardens, take a dip in the sun-warmed pool, and perhaps dive beneath the sea with Jan.

For the past hour she had been in turn despairing of the blow fate had dealt her with regard to her relationship with Reece, and impotently furious with Andrina Saville. Though Reece had explained that there was little he could do she had nevertheless phoned a solicitor to see exactly where she stood. A polite but preoccupied man had informed Juliet that it would be expensive to take proceedings against the accuser, and asked her whether it was really worth it for twenty dollars. It was only then that she had realized the futility of fighting back, and had thrown a few things into her suitcase before despondency took over again.

Now she slipped a flimsy shirt over

her bikini and stood up to answer the knock, knowing the end of her time in Seventh Heaven had finally come and steeling herself for the news of her transfer. It would be back to Spain again, she was certain of it.

When she saw Reece standing there she became confused, agitated and forgot to ask him inside. She stared at him mutely, fixing her compelling gaze on his features, and he met her eyes with equal directness. For a long moment neither spoke. The two of them just stared at each other and Juliet became hotly aware of the sexual charge building rapidly between them. She wrapped the shirt more tightly around her and wished her pulse would slow down.

"Do we have to talk out here?" he said, and only then did Juliet realize that hordes of guests were ambling along the path just five yards from her door as the time-clock in their stomachs told them it was getting on for pre-dinner cocktails.

She dropped her gaze from eyes that burned into hers. "Sorry," she apologized. "I wasn't expecting to see you. Come in."

He followed her inside and when she dared to look up at him again his smile dazzled her. She conquered her immediate impulse to succumb to it and fall into his arms, and reminded herself of her pending transfer.

"Something's happened and I wanted you to be the first to know," Reece explained.

Juliet narrowed her eyes, not knowing exactly what to make of him or of this impromptu visit. She thought she had begun to know him on the island, when the warm, intensely passionate man he was had been revealed to her. Then only a couple of hours ago he had called her into his office, reverting to the former cool, business-like tones and treating her like an employee at a great disadvantage. Now he was showing signs of his alter-ego again. It was unsettling to feel she didn't know him at all. She wished he hadn't come.

"When Mrs Saville accused you of stealing those twenty dollars I hesitated to call you to my office, Juliet." He thrust both hands in his pockets. "The whole thing seemed just too ludicrous for words." His burning eyes scorched her again.

Juliet looked away in confusion. He still wants me, she thought wildly. Despite everything and that awful accusation, he wants us to continue where we left off. And I want that so much, too. But could I do it? she questioned. Could I forget the unfairness of it all? The humiliation? Could I forget the fact that Reece might always harbour a secret suspicion?

As if reading her thoughts he went on. "There was no way I could believe you would steal anything, and my intuition appears to have been right. Mrs Saville found a twenty dollar note half hidden beneath the torn lining of her evening purse. She came to tell me that she has withdrawn her complaint about you."

"She's admitted her error?" Juliet questioned, startled.

"Yes."

"She's apologized?"

Now Reece's smile lit up his face. "You expect too much of the dreadful woman. It's enough, surely, that she has admitted her error and has had the good grace to clear you."

"I can't believe it!" Juliet's spirits surged like a weight suddenly lifted from her shoulders. "You can't imagine how I feel."

"Oh, yes I can. When she first came storming into my office calling for blood it was as if she had accused me personally. I didn't want you to go through such distress, especially with your foot being so painful. But I had no alternative. At the time I don't think you understood my position in the matter."

"I didn't," Juliet admitted.

"When I watched you sitting there

in front of my desk, so vulnerable, so alone, I wanted to reach out to you and tell you that Andrina Saville was nothing but a silly, careless old woman. But she had made a serious accusation that I, as hotel proprietor, could not ignore. Forgive me for being so cold, so insensitive."

"Oh, Reece," she groaned. "I could hardly believe you were being so aloof and distant after . . . after . . . well, after what happened between us on the island . . . "

Her words stumbled to a halt. The sudden memory she had evoked danced tantalizingly between them as the two of them slipped into silence. She could not take her eyes from his face. His bronzed skin was glowing, the lines of anxiety that had shown on his face earlier that afternoon had receded and his grey eyes shone and burned with a passion just waiting to be unleashed.

As she looked at him, secure now in the knowledge that he had always believed her story, she wanted to forget everything that had happened that afternoon and give herself up to rediscovering the strong sexual attraction they held for each other.

"Yes," Reece said, twisting his mouth thoughtfully. "About what happened. Why did you take off like that? Was it something I said? Something I did? I've gone over and over everything. I just don't understand."

Compassion swelled through Juliet. She had a sudden, great belief in the rightness of her instincts and without stopping to consider she reached out, closing the breach between them. She felt a huge tide of tenderness for this man swamp over her, and a sympathy for his confusion and bewilderment.

She raised a hand, pressed her fingers to his lips. She had already decided never to mention her suspicions about him and Koelle. Looking back now everything seemed so trivial. There had been no really positive indications that he was having an affair with her. Juliet considered it had been her own jealous, overwrought mind causing her to act rashly and jump to conclusions.

"No, Reece, of course you won't understand. You're a man. I'm a woman. Women sometimes do silly things that men can't even begin to fathom out."

Cupping his hand around hers he pressed a kiss to her palm. "I'm well aware of that. But I wish you'd tell me and then I'll know never to do or say it again, whatever it was."

Juliet stuck to her resolve. More intensely than she was to ever feel anything again in her life she wanted this man to be happy, to be free from all worries, and she knew that in this respect she could bestow every happiness on him.

"It doesn't matter any more, Reece. It was nothing. Just me being incredibly stupid."

His bemused eyes studied her intently. "Honestly?"

"Yes, honestly. Everything's fine. Just so wonderfully, marvellously fine."

She felt his darkening gaze probing deep within her, searching now for some sign that she wanted to rekindle the raw passion they had ignited the previous day, and she knew with sudden, dizzying knowledge that she was equally empowered to devastate him as he was her.

The sexual charge between them was building into such powerful proportions that it could no longer be ignored. He dropped her hand and she fell against him, daring to unbutton his shirt so that she could achieve the intimate closeness she had craved since the previous day, and press the very essence of herself against him.

He kissed her on the lips until she was dizzy; then he kissed her neck and throat until she thought she might faint with emotion. He pushed the thin shirt from her body and untied the straps of her bikini from around her neck and kissed the golden expanse of flesh across her shoulders. His lips caressed her, his tongue adored her and the erotic thrill of flesh against flesh coursed through her.

In due course he raised his head. Both of them were breathing heavily from the emotional explosion. Juliet felt a measure of triumph at knowing of the effect she had on him. Ever since that embrace on the beach when they had kissed with a wild animal fire she had known how easy it was to entice him. If she wanted to — and she did — she could have seduced him into her bed right there and then. A look, a touch — it would be that easy. She was the sole controller of this situation and the power she held astonished her.

"So," Reece growled huskily, his eyes raking her. "So, what now my love? You know how much I love you, adore you, want you. So where do we go from here?"

Juliet knew what he was hinting at, that he wanted to develop their relationship along more serious lines. But she didn't know what now. She remembered with a sudden sinking heart her transfer request. She uttered a laugh, a giddy, frightened little laugh at the thought of having to leave him and go maybe thousands of miles away. It was too late to cancel the transfer application. Ultimate Tours would already be juggling around their reps in an effort to accommodate her request.

"I've put in for a transfer," she said flatly.

"Yes, I know," he replied, matter-of-factly. Releasing her he dug into his trouser pocket and produced a familiar piece of paper. He stared at it for a moment then groaned. "Oh, my sweet love, were you really going to do it? Were you really going to separate us? For twenty miserable dollars?"

Juliet stared at the paper. "How did you come by that?"

"All things that are to be faxed come through me first. It was on the pile for authorization" — he flicked it between his fingers — "and I rescued it."

"Then — then — it hasn't been sent?"

"No." A mischievous twinkle shone in his eyes. "But there's no problem. It can still be faxed to London if you wish."

"You know I don't want that." She reached out for it, wanting to destroy it immediately. "Give it to me, Reece, so that I can throw it away."

"Not so fast." He snatched his hand away and held the paper high above his head, well out of her reach. "I'll make a bargain with you."

She looked up at him cautiously, questioningly. "What kind of bargain?"

"Marry me," he murmured simply. "And I won't send it."

Juliet dropped her hand and continued to stare at him, held captive by his tantalizing smile. Subconsciously she had somehow known from the day she had first seen him that if she had wanted it — dared to want it — this man could play a vital role in her life. Just how vital, or what kind of role, she had never considered too deeply.

Bewildered now by his sudden and unexpected proposal she blinked, wondering whether it might be a dream and when she opened her eyes he might be gone. But he did not go away. He stood there concentrating totally on her with those intense grey eyes and it became as if they were the only two people in the world — just he, she and a vision of that beautiful house perched on a cliff above a coral-pink beach, with its ocean facing bedroom . . . and a big bed on the main wall . . .

She was suddenly very embarrassed at the unruly course her thoughts were taking and she felt the slow, rosy flush creep into her cheeks.

"So beautiful!" he murmured thickly, his sensual smile widening in wickedness. "You are just so beautiful, Juliet, when you blush and stare at me like that. What are you thinking about?"

She lowered her eyes in case he read the erotic message in them. "You'd be shocked if I told you."

A laugh rumbled softly through him. "I doubt your thoughts are any more shocking than mine. Let me tell you about them. About nights that never end, nights when we'll kiss a thousand times, nights when we'll burn, nights when I'll keep you awake — all night, every night."

A little sound trembled in her throat and she shuddered at the thought of how he meant to keep her awake all night. From beneath lowered lashes she glanced up and saw his eyes burning with a feral-like fire and she was startled to feel an answering heat start to simmer in the pit of her stomach. She felt suddenly very light-headed.

"Hold me, Reece," she breathed. "Just hold me."

His arms automatically went about her again and he pressed her close so that she revelled in the warmth and security of his embrace.

"You really do love me, don't you?" she murmured.

He kissed her tenderly on the top of

her head. "I have no choice. It's what I am."

The feeling of certainty, of serenity that flooded through her was incredible. "It feels so right to be here with you, in your arms, holding each other."

"Then say yes. Please marry me, Juliet. I'll stop at nothing to get you."

She looked up at him, into the tanned face animated now with emotional suspense. His grey eyes could flash fire, they could be as cold as steel, they could speak his thoughts better than words. Right now they were dark with determination.

"Yes, I believe you will."

"So?" he prompted urgently.

His hands were warm, reassuring and strong against her back, his eyes insistent and locked upon hers. Her whole being was leaning towards him, her arm closing tightly around his neck.

"Your body is saying yes, your eyes are saying yes," he murmured. "Will you marry me, Juliet?"

She was becoming dizzy with her own suspense. It was going to be so easy, so wonderful, to love this man. She made her commitment.

"Yes, Reece, I will marry you. Yes!"

His whole body seemed to relax at her words. In a highly symbolic gesture he screwed up her transfer request and tossed it into the waste bin. Then turning back to her he slowly bent his head and took her mouth into his, sealing their promise in a long, meaningful kiss.

THE END

WITH SOMEBODY ELSE
Theresa Charles

Rosamond sets off for Cornwall with Hugo to meet his family, blissfully unaware of the shocks in store for her.

A SUMMER FOR STRANGERS
Claire Hamilton

Because she had lost her job, her flat and she had no money, Tabitha agreed to pose as Adam's future wife although she believed the scheme to be deceitful and cruel.

VILLA OF SINGING WATER
Angela Petron

The disquieting incidents that occurred at the Vatican and the Colosseum did not trouble Jan at first, but then they became increasingly unpleasant and alarming.

DOCTOR NAPIER'S NURSE
Pauline Ash

When cousins Midge and Derry are entered as probationer nurses on the same day but at different hospitals they agree to exchange identities.

A GIRL LIKE JULIE
Louise Ellis

Caroline absolutely adored Hugh Barrington, but then Julie Crane came into their lives. Julie was the kind of girl who attracts men without even trying.

COUNTRY DOCTOR
Paula Lindsay

When Evan Richmond bought a practice in a remote country village he did not realise that a casual encounter would lead to the loss of his heart.

ENCORE
Helga Moray

Craig and Janet realise that their true happiness lies with each other, but it is only under traumatic circumstances that they can be reunited.

NICOLETTE
Ivy Preston

When Grant Alston came back into her life, Nicolette was faced with a dilemma. Should she follow the path of duty or the path of love?

THE GOLDEN PUMA
Margaret Way

Catherine's time was spent looking after her father's Queensland farm. But what life was there without David, who wasn't interested in her?

HOSPITAL BY THE LAKE
Anne Durham

Nurse Marguerite Ingleby was always ready to become personally involved with her patients, to the despair of Brian Field, the Senior Surgical Registrar, who loved her.

VALLEY OF CONFLICT
David Farrell

Isolated in a hostel in the French Alps, Ann Russell sees her fiancé being seduced by a young girl. Then comes the avalanche that imperils their lives.

NURSE'S CHOICE
Peggy Gaddis

A proposal of marriage from the incredibly handsome and wealthy Reagan was enough to upset any girl — and Brooke Martin was no exception.

A DANGEROUS MAN
Anne Goring

Photographer Polly Burton was on safari in Mombasa when she met enigmatic Leon Hammond. But unpredictability was the name of the game where Leon was concerned.

PRECIOUS INHERITANCE
Joan Moules

Karen's new life working for an authoress took her from Sussex to a foreign airstrip and a kidnapping; to a real life adventure as gripping as any in the books she typed.

VISION OF LOVE
Grace Richmond

When Kathy takes over the rundown country kennels she finds Alec Stinton, a local vet, very helpful. But their friendship arouses bitter jealousy and a tragedy seems inevitable.

CRUSADING NURSE
Jane Converse

It was handsome Dr. Corbett who opened Nurse Susan Leighton's eyes and who set her off on a lonely crusade against some powerful enemies and a shattering struggle against the man she loved.

WILD ENCHANTMENT
Christina Green

Rowan's agreeable new boss had a dream of creating a famous perfume using her precious Silverstar, but Rowan's plans were very different.

DESERT ROMANCE
Irene Ord

Sally agrees to take her sister Pam's place as La Chartreuse the dancer, but she finds out there is more to it than dyeing her hair red and looking like her sister.

HEART OF ICE
Marie Sidney

How was January to know that not only would the warmth of the Swiss people thaw out her frozen heart, but that she too would play her part in helping someone to live again?

LUCKY IN LOVE
Margaret Wood

Companion-secretary to wealthy gambler Laura Duxford, who lived in Monaco, seemed to Melanie a fabulous job. Especially as Melanie had already lost her heart to Laura's son, Julian.

NURSE TO PRINCESS JASMINE
Lilian Woodward

Nick's surgeon brother, Tom, performs an operation on an Arabian princess, and she invites Tom, Nick and his fiancé to Omander, where a web of deceit and intrigue closes about them.

THE WAYWARD HEART
Eileen Barry

Disaster-prone Katherine's nickname was "Kate Calamity", but her boss went too far with an outrageous proposal, which because of her latest disaster, she could not refuse.

FOUR WEEKS IN WINTER
Jane Donnelly

Tessa wasn't looking forward to meeting Paul Mellor again — she had made a fool of herself over him once before. But was Orme Jared's solution to her problem likely to be the right one?

SURGERY BY THE SEA
Sheila Douglas

Medical student Meg hadn't really wanted to go and work with a G.P. on the Welsh coast although the job had its compensations. But Owen Roberts was certainly not one of them!

HEAVEN IS HIGH
Anne Hampson

The new heir to the Manor of Marbeck had been found. But it was rather unfortunate that when he arrived unexpectedly he found an uninvited guest, complete with stetson and high boots.

LOVE WILL COME
Sarah Devon

June Baker's boss was not really her idea of her ideal man, but when she went from third typist to boss's secretary overnight she began to change her mind.

ESCAPE TO ROMANCE
Kay Winchester

Oliver and Jean first met on Swale Island. They were both trying to begin their lives afresh, but neither had bargained for complications from the past.

CASTLE IN THE SUN
Cora Mayne

Emma's invalid sister, Kym, needed a warm climate, and Emma jumped at the chance of a job on a Mediterranean island. But Emma soon finds that intrigues and hazards lurk on the sunlit isle.

BEWARE OF LOVE
Kay Winchester

Carol Brampton resumes her nursing career when her family is killed in a car accident. With Dr. Patrick Farrell she begins to pick up the pieces of her life, but is bitterly hurt when insinuations are made about her to Patrick.

DARLING REBEL
Sarah Devon

When Jason Farradale's secretary met with an accident, her glamorous stand-in was quite unable to deal with one problem in particular.

THE PRICE OF PARADISE
Jane Arbor

It was a shock to Fern to meet her estranged husband on an island in the middle of the Indian Ocean, but to discover that her father had engineered it puzzled Fern. What did he hope to achieve?

DOCTOR IN PLASTER
Lisa Cooper

When Dr. Scott Sutcliffe is injured, Nurse Caroline Hurst has to cope with a very demanding private case. But when she realises her exasperating patient has stolen her heart, how can Caroline possibly stay?

A TOUCH OF HONEY
Lucy Gillen

Before she took the job as secretary to author Robert Dean, Cadie had heard how charming he was, but that wasn't her first impression at all.

ROMANTIC LEGACY
Cora Mayne

As kennelmaid to the Armstrongs, Ann Brown, had no idea that she would become the central figure in a web of mystery and intrigue.

THE RELENTLESS TIDE
Jill Murray

Steve Palmer shared Nurse Marie Blane's love of the sea and small boats. Marie's other passion was her step-brother. But when danger threatened who should she turn to — her step-brother or the man who stirred emotions in her heart?

ROMANCE IN NORWAY
Cora Mayne

Nancy Crawford hopes that her visit to Norway will help her to start life again. She certainly finds many surprises there, including unexpected happiness.

UNLOCK MY HEART
Honor Vincent

When Ruth Linton, a young widow with three children, inherits a house in the country, it seems to be the answer to her dreams. But Ruth's problems were only just beginning . . .

SWEET PROMISE
Janet Dailey

Erica had met Rafael in Mexico, where their relationship had been brief but dramatic. Now, over a year later in Texas, she had met him again — and he had the power to wreck her life.

SAFARI ENCOUNTER
Rosemary Carter

Jenny had to accept that she couldn't run her father's game park alone; so she let forceful Joshua Adams virtually take over. But Joshua took over her heart as well!

SHADOW DANCE
Margaret Way

When Carl Danning sent her to interview Richard Kauffman, Alix was far from pleased — but the assignment led her to help Richard repair the situation between him and his ex-wife.

WHITE HIBISCUS
Rosemary Pollock

"A boring English model with dubious morals," was how Count Paul Santana Demajo described Emma. But what about the Count's morals, and who is Marianne?

STARS THROUGH THE MIST
Betty Neels

Secretly in love with Gerard van Doordninck, Deborah should have been thrilled when he asked her to marry him. But he only wanted a wife for practical not romantic reasons.